Praise for *Step to This*

"*Step to This* is a wonderful, w...
laugh-out-loud moments and great lessons."
—Victoria Christopher Murray, author of the
Divine Divas series

"Gia Stokes might be a Hi-Stepper, but this teen role
model has both feet on the ground as she meets life's
challenges with style and grace."
—Melody Carlson, author of the
Diary of a Teenage Girl series

"*Step to This* has alluring characters, wonderful scenes,
and a fascinating premise. Nikki Carter has
a real talent for writing stories that deal with real issues
but are gripping to read by teens and adults alike."
—Jacquelin Thomas, author of The Divine Series

"Filled with smart and witty characters, *Step to This* is a
fun, fast-paced read teens will love."
—Ni-Ni Simone, author of *A Girl Like Me*

"Fun, honest, and so real . . . I loved Gia and cheered
for her as she struggled to find where she fits with
friends, family, and faith. Debut author Nikki Carter is
now on my must-read list!"
—Shelley Adina, author of the All About Us series

"Nikki Carter steps up and delivers a home run with her
debut novel, *Step to This*. It's a real winner."
—Chandra Sparks Taylor, author of *Spin It Like That*
and *The Pledge*

step to this

A So For Real Novel

nikki carter

KENSINGTON PUBLISHING CORP.

www.kensingtonbooks.com

DAFINA BOOKS are published by

Kensington Publishing Corp.
850 Third Avenue
New York, NY 10022

All Kensington titles, imprints, and distributed lines are available at special quantity discounts for bulk purchases for sales promotion, premiums, fund-raising, educational, or institutional use.

Special book excerpts or customized printings can also be created to fit specific needs. For details, write or phone the office of the Kensington Special Sales Manager: Kensington Publishing Corp., 850 Third Avenue, New York, NY 10022. Attn. Special Sales Department. Phone: 1-800-221-2647.

Dafina and the Dafina logo Reg. U.S. Pat. & TM Off.

ISBN-13: 978-0-7582-3439-1
ISBN-10: 0-7582-3439-2

First Printing: March 2009
10 9 8 7 6 5 4 3 2 1

Printed in the United States of America

*To Briana, Brittany, Brynn, and Brooke—
may you always be fearless, fantabulous, and free!*

Acknowledgments

Whew! My first young adult novel ever. I'm so excited!

First, I'd like to thank God for making this possible. I feel truly blessed for this opportunity. Next, I'd like to thank my husband, Brent, for backing me up!

Pattie Steele-Perkins—you are awesome! Thanks for believing in me and taking a chance on this entire project. Thanks also goes out to Selena at Kensington. It's not often that you find an editor who is this excited about a project! I sure appreciate you.

Mercedes Fernandez is getting her own paragraph because she's got it like that! She gets me . . . and trust, that is not an easy thing. So happy Monday through Friday to you, Mercedes, and keep on dancing ☺!

Last but not least, I'm thanking my readers! I hope you enjoy *Step to This* and the many books to come!

Peace—I'm outta here!!
Nikki

The telephone wakes me. Actually, my alarm clock *tried* to wake me, but I hit that snooze button four times.

"Talk to me," I say into the phone in my husky, man-sounding, morning voice.

My best friend, Ricardo, answers. "Gia, wake up. I know you're still in bed."

"How do you know?"

"Because you sound like James Earl Jones. You're going to miss your audition."

"Okay . . . I'm up. See you at school."

I throw my body out of my bed, my feet landing with a *thud*. I don't smell breakfast cooking, so that must mean my mother, Gwendolyn, is out with the street ministry team and I'm on my own.

I open my bedroom door, take two steps, and I'm standing in front of the refrigerator (yes . . . our duplex is that small). Gwendolyn has left me a note. It reads:

God morning, baby. I'm with the evangelism team. Eat some cereal and have a great day.

Why do I have the corniest mother on the planet? She says "God morning" instead of "*good* morning" because, and I quote, "This is the day that the Lord has made. I will rejoice and be glad in it." It's a wonderful scripture and a great thought by my mother, but nobody ever thinks it's funny—not even her friends on the evangelism team.

Gwen will go straight from street witnessing to her job as an LPN at Gramercy Hospital. An LPN is like one step below being a *real* nurse, but my mother couldn't afford to finish the rest of her college degree. She blames that on my deadbeat father, who hasn't paid a nickel in child support since I was a baby. I've only seen him a couple of times, actually, but I don't think it bothers me much. You can't miss what you never had, right?

I think about my audition and feel a little bubble of excitement in the pit of my stomach. My cousin Hope and I are trying out for the Hi-Steppers. It's a drill team/dance squad that is full of the most popular, prettiest, and desired girls in the school.

Hope is one of those popular, pretty, and desired girls. I am their polar opposite.

So why did I let Ricardo talk me into auditioning? Because we will be sixteen this year, and I'm tired of being lame. Don't get it twisted—I'm happy that I have straight A's and proud as I-don't-know-what to be in advanced placement classes, but my social life is the pits.

By the end of this year, my sophomore year, I want to

accomplish three things. First, I need to talk my mother into letting me get a relaxer for my hair. Second, I need to have a guy ask me out on a date, even if my mother doesn't let me go. It would be especially cool if that date was to the Homecoming dance. And third, I need to get a job, so that I can upgrade my entire social situation.

What am I going to wear? After one quick glance around the closet that I share with Gwendolyn, I see it's going to be the usual. A Tweety T-shirt and jeans. Today, I'm going with the red Tweety and faded blue jeans. Hope begged me to borrow one of her little Baby Phat couture outfits for the Hi-Stepper audition, but I refuse to walk up in that piece, sparkling and bedazzled. If they can't see past my faded jeans and Tweety T-shirt, then they are just not ready for me. Plus, Hope only offered her clothes because she's embarrassed of mine.

My cell phone is ringing again. I dash back into my room to answer it before it goes to voice mail.

"Talk to me."

"You really need to stop saying that. It's not cute."

I smile, because I know that my phone etiquette gets on Hope's nerves. I do not care. "Hey, Hope. What's crack-a-lacking?"

"Also not cute. Are you dressed?"

"Somewhat."

Hope sucks her teeth. "That means no. Have you even showered?"

I run down the hallway into the bathroom and start the water. "I will be ready in ten minutes."

"Sure you will. Me and Daddy will pick you up in twenty minutes. Do you want me to bring my flatiron?"

"Nope."

"Well, I'm bringing it anyway."

"I'm wearing a ponytail."

Hope sighs. "It better not be a nappy ponytail, and you better not be wearing one of those Tweety T-shirts."

"Okay! Bye."

I slick my dark pro style gel on the front of my ponytail, tie it down with a scarf and jump into the shower. The warm water feels good splashing my body. I close my eyes and imagine myself wearing that red and black Hi-Steppers uniform and the cute white boots with the tassels on the front. The thought makes me smile.

I can do this.

After my shower is done, on goes my jeans and on goes my boy Tweety. A lot of people think that Tweety is a girl, but he is a boy. Right now, Tweety is my boyfriend. Anyway, I don't care what Hope says, I'm wearing my shirt and I'm wearing my ponytail. I top off my whole look with a short jean jacket and gold hoop earrings.

It's a good look—well, as good as I can come up with on my limited budget.

The horn on my uncle's Benz tells me that it's time to go. I take one last look in the mirror, slick some baby hair (or baby hurrr if you're from the south) on my forehead, and give a little pat to my afro puff.

I'm not really mad at Hope for suggesting that I flat-iron my hair. It always looks great when I do, but my hair is long and thick and as soon as I take one step out the door and into the humidity– it's back to the giant curlfro. So, until I can break Gwendolyn down and convince her that a relaxer is very necessary, I'm rockin' rough and tough with my afro puff.

On the way out the door, I grab a snack-size bag of Doritos. Do Doritos count as cereal? They're made out of corn, so I'm thinking maybe.

I open the door, take a deep breath, and smile up at the sun. Even though it's September, it still feels like summer. All that will change in a month or so, because here in Cleveland we get snow in October.

"Gia! Quit soaking up the sun and come on!"

I squint angrily at Hope, who has her window rolled down and her shiny lips puckered. "I'm coming!"

I run down the raggedy walkway and, as usual, trip over a loose piece of gravel. I don't fall, but I do drop my book bag and spill out some of my folders. I don't know what it is, but lately, I've been super clumsy. It feels like I can trip over air sometimes. It's just something else about me that drives Hope crazy.

Hope gets out of the car to help me. She rolls her eyes at me and says, "Dang, Gia. If you can't even walk to the car, how do you think you're going to be a Hi-Stepper?"

"Whatever, Hope."

I roll my eyes right back at her, snatch my book bag, and get into the car. I could've said so much more than "Whatever." Like the fact that Hope has no rhythm and how she can't even snap her fingers and step at the same time, so how does she think *she* can be a Hi-Stepper? I'm gonna leave it alone, but she better not make me go there.

"Good morning, Gia," my uncle says.

"Hi, Pastor."

Okay, I see the question mark on your face, so let me explain. My uncle Robert is also my pastor. I never call him Uncle Robert, even though he's my favorite uncle. Everybody calls him Pastor Stokes or just Pastor, even my mom, and he's her little brother.

Hope gets back into the car too, and slams her door. "Gia, I thought I asked you not to wear one of those Tweety T-shirts."

Pastor Robert answers for me. "Hope, you are not the boss of Gia. She can wear whatever she wants."

Hope whines, "But, Daddy! She is going to embarrass me. We are trying out for the Hi-Steppers today and she comes out the house looking a mess."

I shout from the backseat, "I don't look a mess!"

"You're right. You don't look a mess—you look a *hot* mess," Hope hisses. "You did this on purpose."

"Whatever, Hope! You act like I'm thinking about you when I pick out my clothes. I'm just that into you, right?" I say sarcastically.

"You *are* that into me! Obviously. You only wanted to be a Hi-Stepper after you heard I was trying out. Why don't you get your own thing?"

"Hi-Stepping is not *your* thing. If you had a thing it wouldn't be Hi-Stepping! It would be looking in the mirror all day counting your pimples!"

Hope cries, "Daddy!"

I can't believe that Hope used to be my favorite cousin. We had "Best Friend" everything—bracelets, necklaces, earrings, folders, and purses. But something happened when we got to ninth grade at Longfellow High School. All of a sudden, she was ashamed to be seen with me because my mom couldn't afford to buy me Baby Phat and Juicy Couture.

The summer before we entered the ninth grade, Hope's mom, Elena, gave her a makeover. She took her to the salon and got her hair straightened and her eyebrows waxed. When my mother saw Hope's new look, all she said was, "She looks grown and fast. No daughter of mine is going to look like that."

I think the fact that I'm growing up scares my mom. She had me when she was seventeen, and she thinks that I might end up like her.

She's got me messed up.

Ain't no way in the world I want a baby or an STD. A sista like me is going to college, for real. You feel me? Plus, I see how hard my mom has it and I'm not trying to go through that too.

Besides, right now, I don't even exist to boys.

I keep wondering when puberty is going to start for me. Hope has been wearing a bra since we were in the sixth grade. I still don't need one, although I wear one on principle. I can't wear an undershirt in the tenth grade.

When we pull up in front of our school, Hope quickly dashes out of the car so that she doesn't have to walk into the audition with me. I fight back the tears that want to come, because there is no way I'm going to let her see how much she hurts me.

Pastor Robert turns around in his seat. "Don't worry, Niecey. I've always liked your T-shirt collection, and your hair is unique. Hope doesn't know everything."

"Thank you, Pastor. See you later, crocodile."

"Bye, alligator."

That's an ongoing joke between us. When I was little I couldn't get that "See you later, alligator, in a while, crocodile" saying right. I always said, "Bye, bye, alligator." My uncle is so cool, even though he is a pastor. He goes out of his way to be a father figure for me because my dad is not around.

As I walk over to the gymnasium, where the auditions are being held, I see my friend Ricardo waving at me. I wave back and smile. Ricardo being there (even though he's supposed to be at football practice) makes me feel so much better.

"Hey, Ricky. Does Coach Rogers know you're here?"

"Yeah, he said it was cool," Ricky replies. "Plus, I'm not starting this week anyway."

"Seriously? Why not?"

He shrugs his broad shoulders. "Some college scouts are coming to see Lance. He could get a scholarship."

Everybody, including Coach Rogers, knows that Ricky should be the starting quarterback for the Longfellow Spartans. But since he's only a sophomore, he doesn't get to play as often as he should. Their senior sensation, Lance Rogers, is the coach's son, so you already know what it is.

"What about the college scouts seeing you?"

Ricky says, "God is going to open a door for me, Gi-Gi. Don't worry about it. Right now, you need to get your head in the game and remember that step we came up with."

Ricardo's older brother, Jordan, is in college and in a fraternity. We used some moves from the Q-dog step show and hooked up a slammin' routine for my audition. Now, I just have to get it right.

Ricky and I walk confidently into the audition. He sits at the top of the bleachers with the other spectators, and I sit in the front row where the other future Hi-Steppers are waiting. Hope pretends to not see me come in.

Hope's friend, Valerie, who is captain of the Hi-Steppers, smiles at me. I smile back and try to make it not look super fake. I know she only pays me any attention because she likes Ricardo. A lot of the girls here are nice to me for that very same reason.

What they don't know is that Ricky would never holler at any of them. He's saved and wants to be a virgin when he gets married, after college. Some girls think that's weird for a guy, but not me. These little trifling girls are always writing notes about the nasty things they want to do to him, but he's not even on that. Plus, two years ago, when he had braces on his teeth, thick glasses instead of contacts, and more bumps on his face than a pizza has pepperoni, none of these girls even said hello. Especially not Valerie.

Hope is the first one up to audition. She hands Valerie a tape with her music on it and then walks to the center of the gym. Hope looks really scared, but she's smiling anyway.

The music starts and Hope does her little routine. It's obvious that Valerie helped her choreograph it because there are a few signature Hi-Stepper moves that Hope could never have thought of on her own. If she smiles any harder I think her face might crack and all her icy pink lip gloss will run down her shirt. Seriously, Hope looks like she tripped and fell lips first into a tub of Vaseline. She finishes and takes a bow, and all of her friends hug her as she comes to sit down.

I've got to admit that it was better than I'd expected. Much better. Hope might actually have the potential of being a decent Hi-Stepper. She gets on my nerves, but I gotta give props where props are due.

After a few really, really bad auditions, it's finally my turn. I give Valerie my tape and walk to the center of the gym with a cane in my hand. The cane was Ricky's idea.

The drumbeat of Destiny's Child's "Lose My Breath" blares from the speakers and I start my complicated routine. My stomps and claps are perfect, and everybody gets pumped when I tap my cane, toss it in the air and catch it with ease.

When I'm done, I get a standing ovation from the entire Hi-Steppers squad. Ricardo is also yelling and clapping like he's lost his mind. This is a good moment—the stuff of legends. Okay, maybe not legends, but it's really, really great!

"**M**om, you should've seen it! I was the best, and Ricky was there too. It was awesome."

"And did you thank the Lord for blessing you with a good audition?"

I bite my lip and bow my head. *I'm sorry, Lord. I forgot to thank you for my good audition. Thank you, thank you, thank you!*

Gwendolyn says, "You should never forget to thank God, even in the midst of excitement. Everything good comes from Him."

"I know, Mom."

Okay, I totally get that my mom is trying to teach me about God. I feel like I was born in the sanctuary, right on the steps where the choir sings. And I *do* love the Lord! Really, I do. But how about her being happy for me? Can I get a congratulations up in this piece? Seriously.

"Gia, I'm on my way to the Singles Ministry meeting. Do you think you can fend for yourself for dinner?"

"Yep."

So it's gonna be a Hamburger Helper night. I'm cool with that. My phone buzzes, letting me know that I've got a text message.

It reads: Congrats! U did a great job

The text message is from Ricky. That's so cool that he remembered.

"No company, Gia, and make sure you're in bed by ten-thirty."

"When do I ever have any company, Mom? That was just so unnecessary."

I watch my mom put on her lipstick, spray on way too much perfume, and fluff out her chin-length bob. Her hair is thick and bouncy—exactly how mine would be if she'd let me use a relaxer.

"Mom, can I go with you to the salon this week? I want to get my hair done like Hope does."

Gwendolyn frowns. "My brother has plenty of money, so Hope can go to the salon every day if she chooses. When the Lord blesses me in my finances, then I'll take you to the salon."

"But what if you don't get your blessing anytime soon? Am I supposed to walk around with this afro puff until I'm grown?"

"We've already had this conversation," she says. "You will only get a relaxer when I have enough money to get it professionally maintained. Otherwise, your hair will end up in a ball on the floor."

I totally have a comeback. "Well, what if I get a job? Then I can pay for it myself."

"School is your job, Gia. You just keep on getting good grades and you're making your contribution to this family."

Since I hadn't planned on the argument going this far, I don't have anything else to say. I should've known she was going to come up with the "school is your job" bit. It's classic parental reasoning. After watching all of *The Cosby Show* reruns, I should've been ready for this.

I'll get her next time.

When Mom is finally dressed and ready to leave, she takes both of my hands in hers. "Come on. Let's pray before I leave."

"Okay."

Mom closes her eyes tightly and says, "Father God, I thank you right now for what you're going to do in my life. Even though these things haven't come yet, I thank you for my husband, Elder LeRon, and I thank you for my financial blessing. Please grant me traveling mercies, as I go to the meeting and return home safely. In Jesus's name."

I say amen even though I don't totally agree with my mother's prayer. I mean, seriously, why would she be praying for a specific man? What if God has someone else in mind? I've asked her about this before, and she says that when we pray we should be specific with God.

I've been specifically praying for a relaxer in my hair, but obviously the Lord is not pleased. Maybe He knows something I don't know. I wish He would reveal it to me, because the press-n-curl Easter hair that I have to wear on Sundays is not a good look.

But anyway, Elder LeRon is so irking. If the Lord answers my mom's prayer, I hope it's after I've already left home for college.

I change my mind about the Hamburger Helper and make myself a grilled cheese sandwich and grape Kool-Aid. Then, I plop down on the couch to finish the geometry homework I started at study hall.

Just as I finish the last problem, my phone rings. "Talk to me."

"Hey, Gia. Did you get my text?"

"Yes, Ricky, I did. Thanks."

"I bet somebody was mad."

I laugh. "Who? Hope?"

"Man, she looked like she was chewing brick potato chips!"

"Yeah, she was salty."

"So, are you coming to the youth prayer on Saturday?" Ricky asks. "Pastor Stokes wants everyone there."

"Of course I'll be there. Gwendolyn would trip if I tried to skip it."

"Good, 'cause everyone's going skating afterward. Kevin is going."

Okay, so I love my friend and everything, but he seriously needs to chill on the matchmaker tip. Kevin is so not the one. He is the opposite of the one. He is the one minus infinity. No.

Kevin is about five feet nothing and has this big old head. He plays tuba in the band. I know, right? So cliché. Plus, he doesn't take a lot of care with his personal hygiene. There's always a ripeness about him that makes me a little bit nauseous.

"Why would I care if Kevin was coming?"

Ricky replies, "Because he told me he likes you. And isn't getting a first date on your list of plans?"

"Well, looks like I won't be getting a relaxer or a job, so why should I get the first date?"

"Why? What's up? Gwendolyn tripping again?"

"You don't even know the half. Anyway, Kevin is a no. I'm not playing, Ricky."

"Well, I think you should talk to my boy. You don't really need a job, and I think your hair is all right, plus dude is really feeling you."

"Next!"

Ricky laughs. "Well, at least you're going to be a Hi-Stepper."

"Yeah, that's true. My show is about to come on, so holla back, okay?"

"Holla."

I hang up the phone and turn on the television with the remote. I never miss an episode of *Smallville* and I'm not about to start tonight, plus Tom Welling is my other boyfriend. It's a repeat, but I'm watching anyway.

Oh, and by the way, did Ricky actually just say he liked my hair? Seriously?

★ 3 ★

It's Tuesday night, and that means youth choir rehearsal night. I love being in the youth choir because, number one, a sista like me can carry a sweet little tune. Number two, we always get to go and minister at places like homeless shelters and teen homes. And number three, the youth choir director, Bryan, has an extra amount of cuteness going on.

After Brother Bryan opens up in prayer, he says, "So, do y'all want to learn a Tye Tribbett song tonight?"

Everyone, of course, screams *Yeah!* We've been trying to get him to teach us something off Tye Tribbett's CD for months. He is our favorite gospel artist, fo' sho'! He gets crunk in his performances too. Of course, that's crunk for Jesus!

Brother Bryan laughs. "Okay, okay! I hear y'all. For youth Sunday next month, I want us to sing 'Seated at the Right Hand of God.' What do y'all think?"

See, I knew me and Brother Bryan were on the same page. That is my favorite song off Mr. Tribbett's album. Maybe that's a sign from the Lord that one day Brother Bryan will be my husband.

What? It could happen!

Hope, who also has a crush on Brother Bryan, whispers to me, "I hope he gives me the solo."

I give her the serious "pump your brakes" side-eye combination. Maybe she had inside connections with the Hi-Steppers, but trust and believe, this solo belongs to *moi*. I am a much better soprano than Hope. There is no way she can hit the high notes on this tune.

"So," Brother Bryan says, "I think we're going to do a duet on this song. Hope will sing the first lead, and then we'll have Gia do the bridge part because she's a high soprano."

This is definitely not the business. I thought me and Brother Bryan were on the same page. Clearly he missed my memo.

That's the one down side about being only Pastor Stokes's niece and not his daughter. Hope always gets extra privileges because she's a PK. That's *preacher's kid* for y'all who ain't seen the inside of a church.

"Thank you, Brother Bryan," Hope gushes.

After rehearsal, Ricky, Kevin, and I stand out in the parking lot chitchatting. We're waiting on our rides. Ricky and Kevin are riding with Brother Bryan and I'm riding home with Hope and my uncle.

Ricky says, "Kev, you should've been at Gia's audition for the Hi-Steppers! It was crazy. If they don't pick her, then somebody is smoking something."

"Thanks, Ricky," I reply.

Kevin scrunches up his nose and frowns. Not a good look. Then he says, "Why do you want to be a Hi-Stepper anyway?"

"Um . . . because it's fun! Cool people like extracurricular activities, Kevin."

"Yeah, Kev," Ricky adds. "Plus it will look great on her college résumé."

"Well," he says with a shake of his head, "only what you do for Christ will last."

Boo, Kevin. Just boo! He's been chilling with his grandparents for too long. He is a miniature, teenaged, old person. Anyway, being a Hi-Stepper doesn't *have* to last. It just has to get me from lameness to popularity. And that is a good look, honey lamb.

Thankfully, Pastor Stokes pulls up to the church door and I hop in the backseat of his Benz. Hope is already in the front. Why does she have on big Hollywood sunglasses like the sun is still out? Utter foolishness, I tell you!

"Bye, Gia! Bye, Hope! Bye, Pastor!" Ricky says with a smile.

I give him the peace sign and Hope acts like she doesn't even hear him. She is beyond ignorant. Pastor Stokes rolls down Hope's window and says, "You two young men have a blessed evening!"

"I'll be praying for your strength, Pastor," Kevin says.

Boo, Grandpa Kevin! Boo!

As we pull out of the church parking lot, Pastor Stokes asks, "So, Gia, how did your audition go?"

"I'm surprised Hope didn't tell you!" I gush. "It was awesome!"

Pastor Stokes looks at Hope and says, "No, she didn't mention it."

"She was all right, I guess," Hope replies. "She won't make the A squad, though."

Oh, no she didn't. I shouldn't be stressed about her hateration, but I can't help it.

"If you make the A squad, then I'm *definitely* making it. My routine was way better than yours," I shout from the backseat.

Hope argues, "Your routine might have been better, but your clothes were lame and your hair was nappy to infinity."

"Infinity? Those flash cards your mother bought you are finally working. Maybe now, they'll let you take classes with the normal kids."

Pastor Stokes intervenes. "Girls, come on now. I'm sure you both did your best, and that's all that matters. And I expect you two to support each other at school and be representatives of Christ and your family."

I sit back in my seat and fold my arms angrily. I blink back the tears that are trying to sting my eyes. Hope is so unnecessarily mean. I know that I can be mean too, but she doesn't even have a reason.

Not a moment too soon we pull into the driveway of my house. Pastor Stokes says, "When you get in there, tell my big sister I said hello."

"Okay," I reply.

I trudge up the walkway and into the house. When I get inside I sling my backpack across the living room and onto our worn-out couch.

"What's the matter with you?" Gwen asks.

"Nothing. Pastor Stokes says hi."

"Hmph. Why didn't he come in and say it himself? Is he too good to come inside our little house?" she asks. "He must've forgotten that I changed his diapers when he was a baby."

I always have to hear how Pastor and his wife think they're too good for this or too good for that. I don't believe my uncle feels that way, but his wife and daughter are a whole other story.

That's all right, though. One day Gwen is gonna find her a husband and come up too. And one day, I'm going to be fly and popular. I just hope it happens soon.

★ 4 ★

Three days have passed since the Hi-Stepper tryouts and everyone is waiting in the hall outside the gym for the list. Hope hasn't spoken to me since this morning, so I guess she is beyond salty. She's standing with her friends Kelani and Jewel, and all three of them are giving me the evil side eye.

I know Kelani and Jewel aren't looking at me crazy! They dress like twins every day, even down to their hair. They tell everyone that they're cousins, even though Kelani's dark skin is the color of a cup of Starbucks coffee and Jewel is like a stick of butter. Today they're wearing twists in their hair with ponytails in the back. Someone should tell Jewel to use the clear gel on her twists, because clumped up brown gel is not a good look in blond hair. Straight lookin' like Ms. Britney Spears when she was going through her "crisis."

"Why does your cousin always wear those busted

T-shirts?" Kelani asks in a voice loud enough for me to hear.

I'd given Tweety a break this morning, but Foghorn Leghorn is in full effect. It's an oversized tee and I've got it tied in a knot on the side.

I know Ms. Kelani doesn't think I'm gonna let that slide. "Whatever, Ke-la-ni! Not everybody's mama bought them a Bedazzler for their birthday."

I was referring to the ridiculous jewel-encrusted jeans that she and Jewel are rocking. I don't care if they do have a designer label on them—they both need to fall back with all that sparkling.

Ricky laughs. "Chill, Gia. Haters gone hate."

"I know but, Ricky, Hope is my cousin. She's supposed to be on my team."

I'll never tell Hope, but I miss how tight we were. It hurts to have her looking at me like an enemy, when I've never done anything wrong to her. I've always had her back. I still have her back whether she wants me to or not.

Finally, Valerie and the rest of the Hi-Steppers march down the hall in full uniform. I think Valerie made a mistake and ordered her skirt a size too small, because it's hiked up in the back by her bodacious booty. Valerie's long, straight brown hair is pulled up into a ponytail on the top of her head and swings back and forth as she marches.

"Ooo-OOO!" Valerie shouts.

"Ooo-OOO!" the rest of the Hi-Steppers call in response, sounding like a flock of wild female birds.

The crowd standing in the hallway parts like the Red Sea, and the Hi-Steppers march down the middle.

Valerie says, "Hi-Steppers, HALT!"

Then, she pulls out a piece of paper. The list. The list that everyone hopes their name is on. I'm trying not to get nervous, but the butterflies in my stomach are dipping, popping, and twerking. For real, though, I can't take the suspense.

Hope doesn't look as nervous as I do. She probably already knows that her name is on the list. That's the only thing it could be, because she couldn't possibly be going on the strength of her wack audition.

"Congratulations to all of the new Hi-Steppers!" Valerie says. "If you didn't make it this year, don't give up. We want to thank everyone for trying out."

As soon as Valerie hangs the list and moves out of the way, the crowd starts to bum rush. The first two girls who look at the list run off in tears, but they both had really bad auditions. The first one tripped and fell in the middle of her routine and the second one did a routine straight out of a T-Pain video. I didn't expect either one of them to make it.

Hope casually walks up to the list, quickly reads it, and then turns to her friends. She's all smiles; she doesn't look surprised at all.

Valerie says, "Congratulations, Hi-Stepper! Ooo-OOO!"

"Ooo-OOO!" Hope responds with a giggle.

Now it's my turn to look at the list. I don't feel the butterflies anymore, but my palms are sweating and my hands are shaking. I feel Ricky's hand on my back, pushing me toward the dreaded sheet of paper. He sure is thirsty to see if I made the team. I don't see him being this thirsty in Coach Rogers's office looking at the football team roster. But I digress.

I scan down the list of names on the A list, which is the starting team. I don't see my name. I feel myself beginning to panic, because both Hope and Kelani's names are right there in my face. And I still don't see my name.

So, I look at the B list, which is the girls who have to go to practice every day, but don't get to perform or even get a uniform. And there is my name. The last name on the B list. I'm on the Hi-Stepper squad, but not really on the squad. Are they serious?

"It's cool, Gia. You made the squad!" Ricky says, ever trying to be the encouraging friend. But right now, I'm gonna need him to chill.

They picked Hope to be a starter and made me a bench warmer? Did they even see my routine? They couldn't have seen it. 'Cause if they had seen it, they would know that not only am I better than Hope, I'm better than half of the squad they already had.

This is so unfair.

Valerie is walking toward me with her arms outstretched and wearing a ridiculously fake smile on her caramel-colored face. She reminds me of a life-size Bratz doll. For real though, I hope she is not trying to get a hug. Oh, but she is, because now her long skinny arms are wrapped around my unresponsive body.

"You had a great audition, Gia!" Valerie gushes. "We're happy to have you on the squad."

"Thank you."

"We only had two open slots for the A squad, but I'm sure that next year you'll move up."

I've got to ask this question. "So, what made you pick Hope to be on the starting squad instead of me?"

Valerie blinks a few times, like no one has ever questioned her before. An uncomfortable smile crosses her face as her eyes dart between me and Ricky. He's staring her down hard too, just like I am.

That's how we do. Bonnie and Clyde up in this piece. She can't step to us!

"Well, it's not just about the routine, mamita," Valerie explains. "It's the whole image. Right now, you don't have the whole package, but I think we can help you with that."

"The whole package? What does that mean?" Ricky asks. I'm so glad he did, because my voice is stuck in my throat.

Valerie tilts her head to one side and replies, "Well, her clothes are not quite Hi-Stepper quality, and her hair leaves something to be desired. You know, the Hi-Steppers are on television once a year for the Friday night game. This year it'll be our Homecoming game, so it *has* to be fly."

"So you're saying my *image* is not ready for prime time?" I ask.

"Right. But it's okay, because we're going to help you become the Hi-Stepper I know you can be. See you at practice."

I turn slowly toward Ricky, trying to contain my rage. "Good night! Did she just say that my image is flawed!"

Ricky struggles for words. "I don't think you're flawed. I think you're fierce."

"Okay, thank you, but I'm gonna need you to never say *fierce* again." I hope that the frown on my face conveys every bit of seriousness. "I am not Tyra, and you are not Mr. or Ms. Jay. For real, though."

Ricky clears his throat. "Never that. I'm just trying to boost up your self-esteem."

Is it me or did Ricky's voice just deepen two or three octaves?

"Who said my self-esteem needed boosting?"

"Nobody. So, I guess we're both riding the bench, huh?"

"Speak for yourself, son."

That's right. Ricky Ricardo is about to be on the bench by himself. Valerie and her robot Hi-Stepper crew just haven't gotten a real taste of my fabulousness. I plan to be front and center when the Hi-Steppers perform on national television. By the end of the year, I'm going to have them all thinking that Tweety and afro puffs are the stuff. For real.

I think.

★ 5 ★

It is nine-thirty in the morning on Saturday, and about ten members of the youth department, me included, have gathered in the church sanctuary for youth prayer. So far, this is not a great turnout, seeing that we have over one hundred young people in our congregation. I expect the late sleepers to start filing in when it's time for the activity portion of the day.

Another unfortunate perk of being related to the pastor is that coming to these things is not optional for me. Pastor Stokes tells me and Hope all the time that we have to be leaders in the congregation and that the young people are watching the decisions we make.

Unfortunately, Kevin is front and center. And can someone tell me why he's grinning at me? I just felt my skin crawl. I say a silent prayer. *Lord, please don't let Kevin say anything to me. I do not want to dog him out in the sanctuary.*

When I open my eyes Kevin is standing in front of me, with his ripeness in full effect. Eww. Double eww.

"Praise the Lord, Sister Gia," Kevin says.

He's still grinning and even worse, he just gave me a saliva shower when he said the *p* in *praise*. Obviously, this must be a test from the Most High, because this is the opposite of my prayer request.

"Hey, Kevin."

"I said praise the Lord, Gia!"

Kevin lives with his grandparents, Deacon and Mother Witherspoon, and he acts as old as they do. All of the old people think that Kevin is great. Me . . . not so much.

"Praise the Lord, Kevin."

He's about to open his mouth and say something else, but Ricardo gets the prayer started. Because Kevin is standing next to me, I get to hold hands with him. Why are his palms so moist? It's hard focusing on the goodness of the Lord with my hand sliding around in Kevin's.

I close my eyes tighter and reflect on the things I need from God. So, I pray for my mom, that she finds a husband and that her finances improve. I pray for wisdom so that I can keep doing well in school, and I pray that Hope and I become real friends again.

After the group prayer is finished, Ricky reads a scripture and dismisses everybody. We're going to IHOP for breakfast and then to the noon skate at the rec center.

Of course, when we leave the church and go into the parking lot, it's full of all the young people who couldn't make it in time to pray. Hope is here and she's invited all of her Hi-Stepper buddies—Valerie, Jewel, and Kelani.

Valerie looks like she's about to audition for *America's*

Next Top Model. I can hear Tyra Banks now, talking about how fierce she looks. Valerie's hair is flatironed pin straight with a slight curl on the end and she has two jeweled butterfly barrettes on each side to hold her thick hair out of her face. She's wearing skinny black designer jeans and a fitted sweater—both items dangerously hugging every curve. She tops off the whole look with black leather boots.

Yeah . . . like I said, fierce.

Ricky walks up to Hope and says, "We missed you this morning in prayer, Hope. Maybe you didn't remember, but it was your turn to lead."

"I know, Ricky, but some of my friends wanted to come to church this morning and we were a little late. Shouldn't we be inviting our friends to church?"

I have to bite my lip to keep from cracking up. I know Hope is not trying to make anyone believe she's out here being a witness for Christ. The very thought of sharing her faith would probably make Hope cringe. More than likely, Valerie and company invited themselves when they heard that Ricky was going to be here.

"Hey, y'all," I say to Hope and crew.

Hope surveys my outfit—a yellow Tweety T-shirt with black baggy jeans—and gives me a tight smile and a nod. Jewel and Kelani giggle like two little hyenas. I want to slap all three of them.

Valerie asks, "Gia, do you want to ride with us to IHOP?"

Hope looks like she's ready to object, but since it's Valerie's car, she doesn't say anything. I don't necessarily want to ride with them, but since my other option is on the church van with clammy-hands Kevin . . . I choose the phony Hi-Steppers.

"Yeah, that's cool." I try to make my reply sound as nonchalant as possible.

We get in the car, and I'm stuck in the backseat between Tweedledee and Twiddledum. Hope sits up front with Valerie.

Before we pull off, Valerie screams out the window to Ricky, "You want to ride with us?"

Ricky smiles shyly. Is he serious with that? "I don't think you all have any room."

"You can sit right here." She smacks her thighs three times and motions to her lap.

Hello! We are in the church parking lot! You do not offer freakiness in the sight of the Lord. I need to get out of this car in case the rapture comes on our way to IHOP.

Ricky shakes his head and walks toward the church van. I find it interesting that he did not seem disgusted at Valerie's antics. He was more embarrassed. And if she can embarrass him, then he *must* like her. Eww. I thought I'd taught him better than that.

Valerie giggles and speeds out of the parking lot. As if on cue, her flunkies, Jewel and Kelani, giggle too.

I have to ask, "What's funny?"

More giggles. They don't know who they are messing with here! They better be glad I just got some prayer.

I lean forward in my seat and speak directly to Valerie. "What is so funny?"

"Fall back, sweetie. Nobody is laughing at your friend. Actually, he's *muy caliente*. He's about to be my boo."

Ha! Did she just call Ricky *hot* like some kind of Latina Paris Hilton? Hilarious. I have to cover my mouth to keep from giggling. There is no way in the world that

Ricky would hook up with Valerie. He might think she's hot, but he's way more grounded than that . . . I think. It's just wrong on so many levels.

But the giggle twins seem to think it's cute and Valerie is convinced.

"Why do you want to talk to Ricky anyway? Isn't he a little bit too lame for you?"

Kelani asks, "You calling your own friend lame?"

Who asked her to speak? I was on a roll. "Anyway," I continue while rolling my eyes at Kelani, "he goes to prayer service on Saturday morning. Just doesn't seem like your type."

"He is my type. I like nice boys too."

"Just not as much as the bad boys," Jewel adds, finally getting in her goofy little two cents.

"Don't try to play my boy, Valerie." I hope that sounded threatening, because I am so not playing.

Hope says with a sneer, "You sound jealous, sweetie. Is somebody crushing on lil' Ricky Rick?"

"I do not like Ricky like that. Please."

Valerie peeks at me through the rearview mirror and smiles. "Good, because Hi-Steppers never share boys. Ever."

With that command, we pull up to the IHOP parking lot. The church van is already there, so clammy-hands Kevin is holding the door for everyone to go through. No, he does not have the audacity to be scowling at me. Does he know who I am?

"What's wrong with you?" I ask him, not really caring about the answer. I just want his one big eye and one little eye to stop looking at me.

He growls, "I saved you a seat on the van, and you never got on."

Dude is really angry. Seriously?

"Sorry, Kevin. I had to ride with the Hi-Steppers. It wasn't personal."

The frown immediately melts from Kevin's face and his scary smile returns. "Well, good. Will you sit with me in the restaurant?"

"Oh, I'm sorry." I bite my lip with fake sincerity. "I already promised Valerie."

I look over my shoulder to locate Valerie and crew. She is still at her car, twirling her hair and batting her eyes at Ricky. While I'm over here having an unnecessary conversation with Kevin the horrible, my best friend needs rescuing . . . I think.

I march over to Valerie's car, gangsta style (all right, not really gangsta, but I'm on a serious mission here).

"Will you guys come on!" I say. "Pancakes are calling my name."

Valerie sashays out of the way so that Ricky can close her car door. I don't dare think this out loud, but Ricky seems mesmerized with all that badonkadunk Valerie's got crammed in her jeans. Her booty is like five of mine. I don't even think I have a badinkadink. So not fair.

I'm feeling something strange—a strong urge to poke a straight pin in Valerie's behind and pop it like a balloon. Is this jealousy? Could it be booty envy? 'Cause I for dang sure am not jealous over Ricky.

Am I?

Okay, I'm practicing this "to mine own self be true" type of thing, and I'm going to be really, really honest. But I'm only going to say this once, and if you tell anybody, it is on and poppin'. Gangsta style.

I kind of like Ricky. Just a little.

There. I said it.

But we've known each other since we were babies. And I *know* for a fact that if he's in a trance over Valerie's body, then he ain't even trying to look at this bag of bones.

So, now that I've put that out there, just tuck it away in your memory bank. You can maybe remind me about it, years from now, if and when my body ever develops past that of a twelve-year-old.

We're all sitting down at a round table inside the restaurant. Kevin somehow squeezed into the last seat next to Hope. I'm between Ricky and Valerie. Yes, doing all kinds of blocking and I am not ashamed.

Hope asks, "Don't you want to trade seats, Gia? Kevin is your boyfriend, right?"

No . . . she . . . didn't.

Oh, I've got something for her.

"Kevin is my friend and Kevin is your friend too, Hope. Don't you remember that time the two of you got naked in Sunday school?"

Ricky and I burst into laughter as does everyone else at the table. That's what she gets for trying to play me.

Hope sucks her teeth and rolls her eyes. "We were three."

"Still, it sounds like he's closer to being your boyfriend than mine."

Kevin drops his head. He is too embarrassed, and now I feel bad. I didn't mean to hurt his feelings, only to get back at Hope. So, I'm going to do the godly, charitable thing.

I say, "But if you want, we can switch seats."

Hope jumps up from the table before I can even finish the sentence. Kevin's face lights up and for a split second, both of his eyes are the same size and he's almost not gross. Ricky smiles at me like he's proud. It's a smile he would give his little sister, or his puppy the first time it went on the newspaper . . . but I'll take it.

The waitress comes around to take our orders. "What y'all havin'?"

I'm so irritated by her three-inch, airbrushed, acrylic nails that I can't remember what I want to eat. Not to mention the huge wad of gum she keeps popping and that three-week-old hair weave she's rocking. She can't be any older than Valerie. Hmm . . . I wonder if she can get me a job up in here.

Valerie asks, "What are your low carb offerings?"

"Um, we have eggs," the waitress replies. "Is that low carb?"

"Yes. I'll have an egg-white omelet with two eggs, please. And these ladies will have the same. We'll also have grapefruit juice."

Kelani, Jewel, and Hope nod. Excuse me! *These ladies!* I hope she wasn't talking about me.

"I'll be having a stack of pancakes topped with apples and whipped cream, please," I say to the waitress as I close my menu with a snap.

Valerie frowns. "Hi-Steppers need a healthy diet. All that sugar and flour is going to bloat you and go straight to your hips."

Hello! How about I want something to go straight to my hips? How about if everything I ate went straight to my hips for the next year, I still wouldn't fill out a pair of jeans like Valerie.

Ricky speaks up. "I'll have the apple pancakes too."

We high-five each other across the table.

"Don't encourage her, Rick," Valerie fusses. "That food is not good for her."

"It's all right. Gia can stand to gain a few pounds."

No . . . he . . . didn't.

I'm just getting played left and right today. From family and friends. And by the way, who is *Rick*? His name is *Ricky*!!!

After we eat our food we all head to the skating rink. I'm looking forward to this, because Ricky and I made up a fresh line dance to do on our skates. We've got a spin and a drop in there . . . it's too for real.

When we step onto the rink, Ciara is blasting from the speakers, telling us she wishes she could be like a boy. I feel her on that.

Speaking of boys, here comes Ricky gliding in his black leather skates like he invented the sport. He's not paying any attention to Valerie and her crew at the skate rental booth, even though Valerie made a point to toss her hair and wiggle herself as he flew by. Just like a boy. Sports come before badonkadunks.

"You ready, Gi-Gi?"

"Like Freddy."

Ricky shakes his head. "So corny."

"I know you ain't talking."

Mario's song "Let Me Love You" comes on, and Ricky and I share a smile. There is no more conversation necessary, because this is our song. Okay, not *our song* like that. This is the song we made our line dance for.

I know what you were thinking. Didn't I tell you to tuck that away?

Anyhoo, we skate out to the middle of the floor and stomp, kick, drop . . . bounce, stomp, twirl . . . clap, kick, bounce. Soon, we have a little crowd, which makes us dance harder. Now, we're popping and locking to the beat of the music, rolling back like we're skating on water.

Hope tightens her eyes and pouts her glossed lips. She's over there hatin'. But her girl Valerie is looking at us with admiration. Like she wants to learn how to skate like this. Well, if she asks real nice, I might teach her a thing or two.

"Rick!" Valerie gushes after our song is done. "That was hot! Do you think you could give me some pointers?"

I guess she wants a different skate tutor. It's all good. I do a little spin and start to backward skate across the center of the floor. I'm not paying attention to where I'm going, because I'm trying to read Ricky's lips. So, the inevitable occurs. I crash, back first into some amateur skater who needs to be in the kiddie circle.

Kevin.

Of course he goes stumbling toward the wall, not even trying to break his fall. It's pitiful and funny. More funny than pitiful. But since I'm a Christian, I gotta go help him.

"T-thank you, Gia," he stammers as I pull him up on his feet.

"Nope, it's my bad. Don't sweat it."

I skate away from Kevin, knowing that he's staring at me, but I don't look back. I'm trying not to sweat some stuff of my own. I mean, for real, I'm trying not to sweat. Moisture and my afro puff do not mix, and as a matter of fact, my slicked down baby hair is going to revert back to its natural state in five . . . four . . . three . . . two . . .

★ 6 ★

"**M**ama, no!"

"What do you mean, 'Mama, no'! Didn't you ask me if you could get a job?"

Gwendolyn has just dropped the bomb of all bombs. I mean it's like Hiroshima up in here. World War II in our living/dining room. She's the U.S. and I'm Japan! She's tripping.

"Yes, but I meant like flipping burgers at McDonald's or a cashier at a supermarket. Not this!"

This is a job reading to and running errands for the oldest, crankiest, meanest, most-evil-eye-giving mother of our church. Mother Cranford. All the young people call her Mother Crabapple.

Gwendolyn shakes her head, dismissing my pain. "Mother Cranford specifically asked for you. I couldn't turn her down."

"Yes, you could've. You could've said, 'Mother, Gia is

so busy with her schoolwork that she has no time for an after-school job.' See how easy that was!"

"Well, it's too late because I've already told Mother Cranford you would do it. She is so excited!"

I'll bet she's excited. Excited like an alley cat that's found a mouse to eat.

"How much am I getting paid?" I ask hopefully.

"Forty dollars a week!"

Why did Gwendolyn say this like she is talking about some real paper? I can't even get one leg of those sparkly jeans for forty dollars. Okay, we know that I don't really want sparkly jeans, but I'm just saying. So much for upgrading my situation.

I'm about to object again when there is a knock on the door. Maybe it's the man from *Extreme Makeover: Home Edition*. I have sent him many letters about this shack that I live in. So far I have not gotten a reply.

Mom looks at herself in the mirror before she goes to the door, like she's expecting someone. She sees me looking at her like she's nuts, so she whispers, "It might be Elder LeRon."

"Why would Elder LeRon be coming over here?"

Gwen smiles and fluffs her hair again. "Because we have a date."

What? So Elder LeRon finally decided to man up and ask my mom out. She deserves it, I guess, but why was I not consulted?

"I'm not sure if I approve," I say with all seriousness.

"Girl, I didn't ask for your permission. *I* gave birth to *you*, not the other way around."

On that note, Gwen sashays herself over to the door.

She didn't ask my permission? Oh, I bet she won't be talking all tough when I tell my uncle she left the house in that snug skirt.

The bright smile on Gwen's face falls right off when she sees that it's just Hope and her mom, Elena. My mom can't stand her sister-in-law, but she loves her pastor/brother to death, so she has to be cool.

"Hello, Elena," my mom says. It sounds like she's got icicles hanging off her tongue. I said cool, Gwen. Not cold.

Aunt Elena ignores Gwendolyn's ugliness and hands her a big garbage bag. "Hello, Gwen."

"What's this?" Mom asks.

"Oh, it's just some things that Hope grew out of. Maybe Gia can use some of them."

Seriously?? They can forget that. I ain't wearing Hope's hand-me-downs. I'll wear the exact same thing every day, seven days a week, all day and all night before I put on any of that mess.

Hope, of course, has to get in a crack too. "There are some cute jeans in there. Mom says my hips are filling out, but you're still straight as a board."

I send an evil glare in Hope's direction. Could this day get any worse? I've got to work for Mother Crabapple and wear Hope's old sparkly jeans?

"We were going to give them to Goodwill," Elena says, "but I said to myself, why do that when we have Gia?"

Apparently, the day can get worse. Jesus take the wheel.

Mom drops the bag on the floor and says, "Gia, we can sort through these later, after we wash them."

Elena responds, "Oh, that's not necessary, Gwen, they're already clean."

Mom sniffs at the bag. "I think they smell a little like mothballs."

Score one for us!! You go, Gwen!

Elena looks at Hope and they burst into laughter. Are they laughing at us, in our own house? They need to fall back, right away.

"Gwen, I'll talk to you later. Enjoy your date with Elder LeRon."

Mom glares at her sister-in-law and says a tight, "Have a blessed evening."

Gwen slams the door and mutters, "How did that heifer know about our date?"

"It's cool, Mom. She's just trying to mess with you."

"Hmph. She better find herself some get right. She don't know who she's messing with up in here."

Gwen sashays right back into her bedroom, probably to pray for some peace in her spirit before her date. I wish she wouldn't let Elena get to her like that. I'll be happy when God blesses my mother with everything she wants, because it's hard to watch her be unhappy.

After a couple of minutes she comes out of her bedroom, looking better than ever.

"You look nice."

"You think so? I hope Elder LeRon thinks so."

"If he doesn't, then bump him. You can do better."

Gwen smiles. "What do you know, girl? Elder LeRon is a good man."

"Well, he ain't all that. He ain't fine!"

My mother can hardly contain her laughter. "Fine ain't everything, Gia. At this point in my life, I want a man who loves the Lord and can take care of us."

Well, she can settle for mediocrity if she wants. When I finally get a boyfriend, he's going to be fine!

There's another knock on the door, and this time it's Gwen's date.

"Elder LeRon! Praise the Lord this evening."

He gives my mom a clean church hug. "Praise the Lord, Gwen. I'm so sorry for being late. I was at the hospital with Pastor Stokes, praying for one of our members."

Gwen smiles and bats her heavily mascaraed eyes. "It's quite all right. Work for the Lord comes before our little dinner date."

Could she be any sweeter? Gag on top of gag.

She turns to me and says, "Gia, aren't you going to speak to Elder LeRon?"

"Hi."

Gwen narrows her eyes at me, and I correct myself. "I mean, praise the Lord, Elder LeRon."

He pats me on my head and replies, "Hey there, young lady!"

Patting me on my head? Seriously? Does he think I'm like three or something?

"Don't wait up for me, Gia," Gwen says. "And don't even think about having company."

I object. "Me and Ricky have a report due for biology."

"Well, it's seven-thirty now. He better be out of my house by nine o'clock. I will be calling to make sure."

Elder LeRon clears his throat. "Are you sure that's wise, Gwen? Teenagers can do a lot in an hour."

"You're right, Elder. Gia, you and Ricky are going to have to study over the phone. Sorry."

Most definitely not appreciating this. He ain't even married my mama yet, and he's trying to put the mack hand down? This is not a good sign.

"Okay, Mom. I'll give Ricky a call."

When they walk out the door I roll my eyes so hard that it hurts. Then I speed-dial Ricky on my cell phone. Yes, I have Ricky on speed-dial. What?

"Hey, Gia. I'm on my way. Have the Kool-Aid ready," Ricky says with a laugh.

"No can do, Ricky. Gwen and her new man think I shouldn't be alone with a boy."

Silence from Ricky. Uncomfortable silence. Me no likee.

Finally, he says, "Are they serious? We're like cousins."

Cousins? Okay, I guess I should be glad he didn't say I was like his little sister. That would be even worse.

"Yeah, they're serious. But we're done with our report anyway. We were just going to be chillaxin' and drinking Kool-Aid."

My other line clicks. "Hold on a sec, Ricky, somebody's on my other line."

"Maybe it's Kevin."

"Shut up, boy."

I click over and say, "Talk to me."

"Eww . . . please stop that." It's Valerie.

"Oh, hi, Valerie."

"That foolishness almost made me forget why I called you. I'm having a sleepover Saturday night, and you're invited. Hi-Steppers only, so don't bring any of your little friends."

I'm a little bit excited because I've never been invited

to a sleepover before. Hope doesn't count because she's my cousin.

"Cool, Valerie. I'll be there."

"Good. Holla!"

I click back over to Ricky. "I'm going to a sleepover at Valerie's house."

"Aren't you getting popular?" he asks with a giggle.

"Looks like it."

Still laughing, he says, "Party at Valerie's house. Can I come?"

The fact that he even asks this, jokingly or not, is so not cool. I'm mad that my friend is digging on Valerie, because she (inflated booty and all) is not the one.

"Why, Ricky? You like her or something?"

"Nah, she's not my type."

He needs to stop playing! Valerie is every boy's type.

"I can't tell, the way you're all up in her face."

Do I sound jealous? I hope not.

"Dang, Gia. You my mama or something?" Ricky asks.

Ouch. Not the mama!!! "I'm just messing with you, Ricky. Or should I say Rick?"

"Don't call me Rick. My name is Ricky."

We both laugh at this. So, okay, maybe I haven't lost my friend to the dark side that is Valerie and her tight jeans. Thank you and amen!

★ 7 ★

Tonight is Thursday night skate at the recreation center and Gwen lets me go when I don't have any homework, tests, or any church events. Ricky and I like to go to this session to practice and perfect our steps.

"So what song are we gonna step to?" Ricky asks as he does a half twirl to warm his skates up.

I ponder for a moment and then reply, "I'm really digging those Ciara cuts right now. How about 'One, Two Step'?"

"You *would* pick that song. What is that, the Hi-Steppers' anthem or something?"

"Ha! It would be if we had any *real* steppers. You should see the atrocity that they've put together for tomorrow's game."

Last school year, the highlight of the football game was not the winning score or someone returning a punt for a touchdown. The highlight of the game was the halftime

Hi-Steppers' performance. But the main choreographer graduated and now Valerie and company are struggling to come up with hot material.

"What are y'all stepping to?" Ricky asks.

"Do you mean what are *they* stepping to? Another Ciara joint. 'Oh.' "

Ricky laughs. "Dang! Y'all love some Ciara."

"Yeah, they do."

"Why do you keep saying *they* like you're not a Hi-Stepper?"

I poke my lips out and frown. "Because technically, I'm not a Hi-Stepper. I'm just chilling on the bench in that crazy red jogging suit. I'm tempted to quit the squad, because I could be spending my time doing something else."

"Wow, Gia. I never thought I'd hear that coming from you. Do you think I feel like I'm not a part of the football team just because I'm riding the bench?"

"You *should*! It's not fair that you've got to sit on the side with the cheerleaders, especially when you're the best one on the team."

Ricky sits down on the bench and I take a seat next to him. He says, "On the real, I do get bummed out sometimes about not starting. I talked to Pastor Stokes about it."

"For real? What did he say?"

"He told me that when God gets ready to open a door, no man can shut it. He also said that I'll have my time to shine."

"Pastor Stokes be spitting knowledge."

Ricky lowers his eyebrows at me and then bursts out laughing. "Gia, you sound crazy trying to talk hood! Pastor Stokes *be* spitting knowledge? Oh my goodness."

After a half second of being offended, I join Ricky in his laughter. He's right too. It's very hard for me to use slanguage without sounding lame. Maybe, it's because I have too many over-three-syllable SAT words in my vocab. Don't hate a sista 'cause she's college bound!

"What are you two laughing at?" Valerie asks.

Ricky and I immediately snap out of our giggle fest. Valerie is standing in front of us wearing a tiny jean tennis skirt and a cute Baby Phat T-shirt. Her hair is pulled up in two bouncy ponytails. And why does this heifer smell like a whole bag of peach Jolly Rancher candy?

Ricky is just plain mesmerized, sitting with his mouth hanging open. I want to smack him right upside his acorn head.

"When did you get here?" Ricky asks.

Valerie licks her lips and then smiles. "I just got here."

She needs to simmer down with all that lip licking. I ask, "What made you come up here tonight? You're never here on Thursdays."

"I just wanted Rick to give me some skating tips. That step you two did last week was off the chain."

Ricky stands up and takes Valerie by both hands. He says, "Come on! I'll show you how to backward skate."

"Backward!" Valerie exclaims. "I don't know if I'm ready for all that! I'm still getting forward down."

Ain't this about a monkey's uncle? Somehow, I thought Ricky and I were about to make up our step. But judging by the tee-hee-heeing going on between him and Valerie, it's obviously not going down like that.

Since I'm clearly being ignored, I skate over to the concession stand to get myself a sweet and tasty beverage. A cherry Slushee to be exact. Maybe I'll get a couple of Laffy Taffy's too.

I skate past some of the football players from school. I consider waving to them, but I doubt if they even know who I am. They're sitting next to the concession line, so since I'm not going to speak, I look away and try to pretend like I didn't see them. But I stand close enough to hear their conversation, because I'm just nosy like that.

One of them says, "Valerie's looking hot tonight, man. Did y'all see that little skirt? That little mami is off the chain."

"Yeah, but she's drooling over that lame Ricardo," a player named Romeo says.

I know his name because everybody knows Romeo. He is one of the finest boys in school. He plays tailback on the football team. He looks like a six-foot-tall Bow Wow, with big beautiful eyes and perfectly unchapped lips. He's always fresh and clean too—never ripe like Kevin.

The other player replies, "Ricardo? I thought he was kicking it with that skinny girl."

Romeo laughs. "Nah, she's like his little sister or something. I think they go to church together."

What! They know me? Well, no one actually said my name, but they know who I am! Wow. I didn't know that I even existed outside of my circle.

But why I gotta be "that skinny girl"? Ugh!

Romeo takes a sip of his Slushee and says, "She is skinny, but she's got a cute face."

"Man, I need a thick girl like Valerie," Romeo's homeboy says.

Oh. My. Goodness.

Did I just hear the finest boy in the school say that I have a cute face? Get the heck outta here. Maybe there is a come up in my future.

After I get my Slushee, I stand on the side wall and watch the action on the skate floor. My eyes can't help but wander over to Ricky and Valerie. My eyes also can't help rolling at the sight of her antics.

Valerie is flailing her arms all over the place and nearly falling with every step. Of course Ricky, being the gentleman that he is, helps her up and tries to steady her. When she starts to fall again he grabs her around her waist from the back. And no this dude did not just look at her booty! He gets on my nerves. And so does Valerie and all her "thickness."

I finish my Slushee, toss my cup in the trash can and head back to the skate floor. Ricky pulls Valerie over to where I am, and they're both still giggling. Yuck. I'm throwing up in my mouth right now.

"Gia, you can have your skating partner back now. I'm done!" Valerie says.

Wow. She's going to let me have my friend back. Just wow.

Ricky helps her onto the carpet. "She did a good job, Gia. Soon she'll be making up steps with us."

If by soon he means after hell freezes over, cows jump over the moon, and pigs fly, then I agree.

I don't reply to Ricky's irritating comment, nor do I acknowledge Valerie giving me my friend back. I will not dignify any of this foolishness with a response.

Right before I get ready to skate away from them, Valerie says, "I saw you over there looking at Romeo. You feeling him?"

Ricky bursts into laughter. "Romeo! Puh-lease. She is not feeling him. Nah."

"Thank you, Ricky, but I can speak for myself. Valerie, Romeo is a cutie, but I don't really know him."

Valerie smiles. "Do you want to know him?"

"Does he want to know me?" I ask. "Because I don't chase boys."

Valerie high-fives me. "Ooo-OOO! That's true to the Hi-Stepper game! I heard that. Make them dudes chase you, mami."

Valerie sees her cronies, Jewel and Kelani, and skates off to meet them. Ricky is standing here looking at me like I'm crazy.

I ask, "What is your malfunction?"

"What is yours? Since when did you think Romeo was a cutie?"

"Uh . . . none of your business! I don't tell you *every-thing,* Ricky," I reply as I skate to the middle of the floor.

Ricky follows me. "Yes you do! You do tell me everything, or you used to. What's up with that?"

How about he never told me that he would go ga-ga over a big booty and a smile! It seems like I'm not the only one keeping secrets. What's up with *that*?

Mommy, how was your date with Elder LeRon?"
I already know the answer to this question because Gwen got in too late to join her friends on the
evangelism team the morning after. Plus, she's around
here singing. And trust, Gwen cannot sing a lick.

Gwen drops her eyebrows and twists her lips to the
side—this is her suspicious face. " 'Mommy'? What's gotten into you? You must want something."

There's no fooling Gwendolyn, not today, so I might as
well just spit it out. "Well, I've been invited to a sleepover, and I really, really, really want to go. Mommy . . .
please?"

"Whose sleepover is it?" she asks, hands on her hips in
full-blown interrogation mode.

I reply in a whisper. "Valerie's."

"Valerie who? Do I know her?"

"She's the head of the Hi-Steppers and we're gonna be

choreographing the step routine for the Homecoming game."

This information means nothing to Gwen. Her rules about sleepovers are pretty strict. If it's not family, she's got to know their mama, daddy, aunties, what church they go to, their GPA. . . . You get my point? I might as well be asking to go on a spaceship to the moon.

"What church does she go to?" Gwen asks.

"I'm not sure."

"Well, is she even saved? Do you know that much?"

"She came to our last youth prayer." Technically, this is true. Gwen doesn't need to know that she only came for IHOP and Ricky.

Gwen considers this for a second. "Are there going to be any boys?"

"No! It's for the Hi-Steppers only."

Okay, so I can't say for sure that there won't be boys. But so what? I'm a good kid and I've got my own mind. No one can convince me to do anything I don't want to do. I just wish my mom could see that.

When she still hasn't said yes, I pull out the desperation card. "Hope is going."

"Well . . . I guess if Hope is going." Gwen is breaking down! "You can go. But only after you see Mother Cranford."

Aw, man. I forgot all about Mother Crabapple. I guess Valerie will just have to pick me up from there.

Later, at school, I'm in too good of a mood.

"So did Gwen say you could go over Valerie's house?" Ricky asks as we stand at my locker before first period.

"Yeah, but I gotta go see Mother Crabapple first."

"Bummer. You want me to go with you?"

What? My face is totally twisted with confusion. "You mean over to Mother Cranford's?"

"Yeah. We haven't been hanging out much lately with football and the Hi-Steppers."

What is wrong with my boy? He always goes to the recreation center on Saturday afternoons. We both go, actually. It's the spot.

"So you're saying you would rather go over some old church mother's house than kick it at the rec center?"

Ricky laughs. "No. I'm saying that I want to kick it with my best friend."

I narrow my eyes and stare Ricky down. He is so not fooling me with this mess. Does he know who I am?

"This doesn't have anything to do with you sneaking a peek at Valerie's booty when she picks me up, does it?"

"All right. You got me."

I hit Ricky in the head with a ruler. "Dang, Ricky! Why don't you just admit that you like her?"

"Because I'm not supposed to like girls like Valerie. But I can't help it. She's got me open."

"So why'd you lie to me?" I ask, feeling so betrayed by my boy.

Ricky crosses his arms. "You want the truth?"

"The whole and nothing but."

"I thought you might be jealous."

Let's clarify something. I *am* jealous. But am I about to let him know that? Heck to the nizzo.

"Why would I be jealous? I don't care who you like."

Ricky looks relieved. "I'm glad, because I've been wanting to talk to you about this."

I give my boy a friendly, cousinly hug. "Real talk. You can tell me anything, Ricky."

Ricky opens his mouth like he's about to say something sentimental, but Valerie steps up from out of nowhere, totally wrecking his flow. Straight hater move.

"Good morning, Hi-Stepper!" Valerie says as she squeezes between me and Ricky.

"What's up, Valerie?"

Valerie touches Ricky on the cheek. "Hello, Rick."

"Umm, hi, Valerie," Ricky says nervously. "How's it goin'?"

How's it goin'? Boo is losing all kinds of cool points dealing with Valerie.

Valerie replies, with a seductive smile, "Today is going well. Thanks for asking."

She holds Ricky's gaze for a moment, just to make sure all eyes are on her. Then she snaps her attention to me, all the while giving Ricky a nice view of her bootay.

"Lunchtime rehearsal today, Gia. We've got a game tonight and we need to tighten up a few things."

Actually, they needed to tighten up more than a few things. Number one on the list is Hope and her non-steppin' self. She's been learning the same routine for two weeks and still doesn't have it down.

"Okay. I'll be there."

Valerie walks away slowly, clicking her stiletto heels as she goes. Can I ask who in the world wears stiletto heels to school? This chick thinks she's Jessica Alba or somebody. But Ricky seems to appreciate it because his breathing is fast and shallow like he's about to have a heart attack or something. I mean, dang, she ain't *that* fine.

I tap Ricky on his shoulder to snap him out of his trance. "You're just pitiful. You know that, right?"

"I'm sorry, Gia. That girl is a dime and some change. For real."

Okay, y'all might think that what I'm about to say is a hater move. But trust, it's not.

"Ricky you don't want to get gone off of Valerie. She's just going to hurt you."

He laughs. "Hurt me? Nah, it ain't goin' down like that."

"I'm just sayin'."

"Thanks for looking out for me, baby girl, but I got this."

"All right then."

Who is this slang-talking Ricky who likes big booties and calls me baby girl? I don't know him anymore. He tries to be smooth as he walks away, but his inner lame escapes when he high-five's Kevin on the way to class.

I like the old Ricky with his corny jokes, leading the youth prayer and slipping a random fierce into conversations. I hope he's not trying to change for Valerie. Rick can go on somewhere. Bring back Ricky.

I sit through geometry, ace my world history exam, and harass Ms. Leiman in French class. Well, everyone harasses poor Ms. Leiman. She tries to make everybody use only French during class, but no one listens. Half of these fools can't even count to ten in French, much less construct a sentence. As a matter of fact, Romeo just asked if he could go to "le bathroom." Ms. Leiman looks like that little vein is about to pop on the side of her fore-head. She takes a swig from her coffee cup and swallows hard. Then she writes Romeo a hall pass with the frown still on her face.

On his way out of class, Romeo winks at me and says, "How you doin', shorty?"

"Hey, Romeo," I reply, sounding totally lame.

When did I become a shorty? I didn't know I had been upgraded. And did I mention how ridiculously fine Romeo is? I'm sure I mentioned it before, but I thought I'd just remind you.

I feel my hand reach up to pat my afro puff and straighten out my Tweety shirt. Then I let my mind wander a little. What if Romeo is my first date? That would be too for real.

I'm still on a Romeo high when I go to meet the other Hi-Steppers in the courtyard at lunchtime. Valerie and Hope are already there and Valerie is trying to help Hope with this little rocking move like Ciara did on the "Oh" video.

Hope so doesn't have it.

"Let me help," I offer.

Hope rolls her eyes as I nail the move. If only I had Ciara's curves, I'd be killin' 'em.

"See, Hope," I say, "you've really got to put your weight into it. Just step out and let your hips roll, but keep your back straight while you do it."

Hope keeps rolling her eyes at me, but she tries again and kind of gets it right. Yeah, I said *kind of*. I don't see how the two of us can be related. Hope has absolutely no rhythmical skills whatsoever. She must take after her mother.

Valerie says, "Hope, you better listen to your cousin or you're going to be riding the bench, sweetie."

By then all the other Hi-Steppers had arrived and they're snickering and giggling at Hope. They sure are an evil group of girls. I mean, this could easily be one of their non-steppin' behinds. I feel kind of bad for my cousin when her eyes get all watery.

I whisper to her. "Don't cry, Hope. I'll help you learn it."

"I don't need your help," she hisses angrily, and then pushes me out of her way.

Well, bump her then! I'm just trying to help her re-tarded non-steppin' self. Now I'm going to just let her look foolish.

Hope struggles through the rest of the rehearsal. She's a soldier though, because she doesn't quit at all. She even stumbles to the ground on this tricky crossover move, but she hops up quicker than Michelle from Destiny's Child that time she fell during a concert. Valerie did give Hope the evil side eye, though, just like Beyoncé did to Michelle.

At the end of practice, Valerie pulls me to the side and says, "Why don't you let me give you a makeover? I could hook you up, and you might just end up on the A squad."

"A makeover? I don't need a makeover."

Okay, perhaps I do need a makeover, but I don't know if I want to admit that to Valerie. This is the chick who fixed her mouth to say that my image was flawed.

"Gia, stop playing. You do need a makeover, ASAP. I

can get you a cute ponytail and I've got some clothes you can fit into."

I'm seriously on the fence here. "I don't know, Valerie. I like my look."

"What look?" Valerie says with a laugh. "Tweety T-shirts and jeans is not a look. And if it is a look—it's not a good look."

I get ready to object, but Valerie continues. "Plus you'll never pull Romeo looking like that."

Dang, news sure travels fast around here. Talk about warp speed.

"Who said I wanted to talk to Romeo?"

"Girl, please. You know you like him. And I just happen to know that he called you a 'diamond in the rough.' He's so poetic."

I nod my head. "Yeah. He's a real Langston Hughes."

"Who?"

"Never mind. I'll think about it, Valerie."

"Think long . . . think wrong, boo."

Now that was just wrong. Wrong on so many bad sports, gangsta, and mafia movie levels.

But, time for some real talk. A sista like me is definitely trying to get a starting spot on the A squad. (I would look sick to death in those white boots.) Even if it means that I have to let Valerie make me over like a lifesize Bratz doll, and even if it means Hope is going to the bench.

So, here's the thing. I see what's in it for me. What's in it for Valerie?

★ 9 ★

I'm sitting in the stands at the football game, looking right crazy in a red jogging suit, when Hope and the rest of the Hi-Steppers strut by in those fly white boots. I know their step inside and out, and I do it better than every single last one of them. It is so not fair, but I'm trying to keep Ricky's pep talk at the front of my mind.

I catch a glimpse of Hope's face and she looks scared. She should, because she's in serious danger of making a fool of herself tonight. I hope she had her daddy pray for her before she left the house.

Before we came out on the field, everyone was in the girls' locker room getting ready for the game. Valerie gave a speech to the Hi-Steppers and it was not pretty. Not at all.

After she was done with her speech, Valerie backed Hope up against a locker with her pointy fingernail. "Hope, you better not screw up tonight. Don't make me regret putting you on the A squad."

"I've been practicing, Valerie. I won't mess up." Hope's voice had trembled like she didn't believe it herself.

"You better not," Valerie threatened, while Kelani and Jewel snickered.

Valerie then turned on dumb and dumber and said, "What are you two laughing at? I don't know what kind of squad we have this year! Most of y'all got two left feet and can't step. Gia be making all of y'all look stupid in practice."

I hadn't known how to take the backhanded compliment. It was true, though. I *did* learn the steps quicker than everyone else, but I felt bad for Hope.

As the Hi-Steppers lined up, I touched Hope on her back, trying to give her some of my confidence, but she just rolled her eyes at me. I don't even know why I keep trying to be nice to her; everytime she just does something to hurt my feelings.

Anyway, now we're out here standing in the cold. I would be colder if I was wearing the Hi-Steppers miniskirt, shiny stockings, and boots, but I would so not care. I'd freeze my butt off and be smiling all the way.

I glance down and see the football teams clear off the field for the halftime show. Ricky is sitting on the bench, fully dressed in his uniform that never gets dirty. He looks up at me and I wave at him. He smiles and waves back.

I'm about to holler something in his direction when Valerie ooo-OOO's her way past him, popping that booty extra hard. That fool is looking straight hypnotized. Y'all know how Homer Simpson looks when he's about to eat a donut? Well, that's how Ricky was just drooling over Valerie.

The Hi-Steppers follow the band onto the field for the halftime show. They're playing something that sounds like it's supposed to be a Chris Brown song, but our band isn't that good. The drums sound tight though.

Then, the flute section starts to play the introduction to "Oh" by Ciara and the Hi-Steppers stand at attention. All the girls roll their hips to the right, then to the left. Next, they do the little rocking move that Hope didn't have down in practice.

Guess what? She still doesn't have it down.

She's about a half second behind the rest of the girls and it looks a mess. As they transition into the next move, she's still behind and Jewel trips over her foot. The whole left side of the Hi-Stepper line is looking foolish now, and there's no recovering from that.

Thank the Lord, the song finally finishes and the Hi-Steppers march off the field. Valerie is looking all kinds of angry, and Hope has tears streaming down her face. Dang, that's messed up. Even though Hope has been so mean to me, she doesn't deserve this. I wouldn't wish this embarrassment on my worst enemy.

During the second half of the game, the Longfellow Spartans do just as badly as the Hi-Steppers. So-called star quarterback Lance Rogers throws an interception and gets sacked four times. Coach Rogers is looking real salty, especially with all of those college scouts in the stands, but that's what he gets for not starting Ricky.

Win or lose, the team always goes to IHOP after the game, and of course the girls follow. It's like a Friday night ritual. It's where all the hookups and breakups happen, and where all the good gossip gets shared.

Since I'm a Hi-Stepper now, I've got to make an appearance, but if I walk in the house after eleven o'clock, I can forget about Valerie's sleepover. Gwen does not play when it comes to curfew. I'm lucky she doesn't still make me come in the house when the streetlights go on.

I walk into the restaurant with the rest of the Hi-Steppers, minus Hope. She went home right after the game, because Valerie was giving her the silent treatment. And of course that meant the dummy twins weren't talking to her either.

We're all wearing our red jogging suits now, because the skirts and boots are only for the field. The good thing about this jogging suit is that it's baggy enough to hide my skinny arms and legs. Tonight I've got two afro puffs with red ribbons tied around them. My bubblegum lip gloss is poppin' too, right along with my hoop earrings.

Still, I'm no match for Valerie, who is wearing a bouncing and behaving ponytail. She's got a line drawn under her eyes with the black face paint that the football players use. I wish I'd thought of that first, because it's actually kind of hot.

Jewel, Kelani, and I sit at the same table, while the older Hi-Steppers snuggle up with their boyfriends. Valerie sits down next to Ricky. He tries to act all cool, like it's no big deal, but I can tell he's stressing. I roll my eyes at him and try not to look in their direction.

"Why you lookin' all evil, lil' shorty?" Romeo asks.

I was so busy paying attention to Ricky and Valerie that I hadn't even seen him walk up. He pushes me over in the booth with his hips and invites himself to our table. Kelani and Jewel immediately start grinning.

"I'm cool," I say, also trying to act stress-free. "I just wish y'all had won the game, that's all."

"Who you telling!" Romeo says. "We keep playing like this we ain't gonna see the play-offs this season."

I guess Romeo thinks that I don't notice his arm perched up on the back of the booth. He's tripping if he thinks he's about to put his arm around me. It ain't goin' down like that. But isn't that awesome that a boy is trying to put his arm around me? I mean, Romeo is extra fine.

I lean forward and say to Jewel, "Maybe they would win if they let my boy Ricky start instead of butterfingers Lance."

Jewel laughs. "Seriously!"

"Y'all don't know nothing 'bout no football," Romeo says. "Y'all just keep making up those little dance steps."

"Whatever." I roll my eyes even though I'm grinning from ear to ear.

Romeo asks, "What happened to the Hi-Steppers tonight? If we looked a mess on the field, y'all was extra messy. Did y'all practice?"

"Um . . . that was Hope and her two left feet," Kelani says.

"Yeah," Jewel adds, "I don't even know why Valerie put her on the squad."

I clear my throat and look away because I am totally uncomfortable with this conversation. Also, I'm trying to ignore the Vaseline on Jewel's forehead. It looks like she tried to give herself some baby hair. Yeah, just imagine that and take a mental picture with it.

"Y'all can simmer down with all that talking about my cousin," I say, but I'm not sure if I sound like I really mean it.

The waitress walks up to our table with a real irritated

look on her face, like she hates waiting on a bunch of kids who don't know anything about leaving a tip.

"What can I get y'all?"

Romeo speaks up. "We'll all have some hot cocoa."

"Four cocoas. Anything else?"

"You want some apple pie, lil' mama?"

I nod my head slowly because no sound is coming out of my mouth. I feel like I'm in the *Twilight Zone* or something, with all this lil' mama this and shorty that. I mean—real talk—there weren't any boys checking for me a week ago, especially not a hottie like Romeo.

Ricky must be getting a strange vibe from Romeo too, because he untangles himself from Valerie and starts over to our table. Valerie crosses her arms and pouts angrily, but Ricky doesn't look back.

"You want me to walk you home, Gia? Gwen is gonna be tripping in a minute."

Romeo frowns. "Man, quit blocking. She ain't even had her cocoa yet."

"He's right, Romeo. My mother is nothing nice when she's angry. I'm not trying to get grounded."

"Well, I don't want you to get grounded either. Especially, since I was planning on asking you to go to the movies tomorrow."

I can't stop smiling now. "You were?"

"Yeah, shorty. You down?"

I open my mouth to answer, but Ricky beats me to it. "She's got to go over to one of the church mother's houses tomorrow, and then to a slumber party at Valerie's."

Now Ricky's trying to spill out my whole life's itinerary. He and I are going to have a serious talk about his unapologetic blocking.

"He's right," I finally say. "But what about Sunday afternoon? After I get out of church."

Romeo smiles. "Fo' sho'. Meet me at the mall at four o'clock. We can get something to eat and then catch the five-thirty show."

"All right then," I reply, trying to sound like I'm not stressed at all. But on the real, I've never been more stressed in my life.

Valerie calls to me and Ricky as we head for the restaurant door. "See you tomorrow, Hi-Stepper! Ooo-OOO!"

"All right then, Valerie." Ricky walks back and gives Valerie a brief hug.

Valerie grabs Ricky's arm as he tries to pull away and whispers loudly in his ear, "See you later, Rick."

Ricky bites his lip like he's thinking of staying. And did he just shiver? Valerie's got him open, and it's not cute. Not even a little bit.

We walk in silence down the street toward me and Gwen's apartment. It's only a few blocks away, but we need to hurry. Ricky seems to be deep in thought about something. He's got his hands crammed in his pockets and his eyebrows are furrowed into a deep frown.

Suddenly he asks, "Do you like Romeo?"

"I don't really know him yet," I say dismissively. I don't know if I want to have this conversation with Ricky. Not after how he acted at IHOP.

"Well, I do know him. He's not a nice guy."

I can't tell if Ricky is blocking or if he's being real. "Well, you know I like to judge people for myself."

"He never kicks it with girls like you, Gia," Ricky says, like it's a hard and fast fact that can't ever be changed.

I stop walking and put one hand on my hip, 'cause I'm starting to get heated. "Girls like me?"

Ricky lets out a frustrated sigh. "You know what I mean, Gia."

"No, Ricky. Tell me what you mean."

"It's just that . . ."

I toss one angry hand into the air and start storming down the street. I mean, I know I'm not fly like Valerie. I don't need Ricky to tell me that. But I am cute and funny and cool. Just because Ricky only cares about fat booties, it doesn't mean that Romeo can't like me.

Ricky's supposed to be my best friend! He knows what a great person I am, so it really hurts for him to think that I'm undatable and unlikable.

Ricky runs to catch up with me and says between breaths, "I—I'm sorry, Gia. There is no reason why Romeo wouldn't want to talk to you."

"And?"

Ricky places a hand on my shoulder. "And, you're afro puffs are the stuff, Tweety is off the chain, and you are a much better stepper than Valerie and her whole crew."

I smile up at him. "You don't mean it."

"I do too. Now let's get moving, before Gwen knocks your head off."

Ricky takes off running down the street and I give chase. I'm almost as fast as he is, so I guess these skinny legs are good for something.

Ricky beats me to my house. He yells, "Come on slow-poke!"

I punch him in the arm when I finally make it to my door. I use my key, and Ricky follows close behind. He always has to make sure I get in safely.

Gwen is sitting on the couch with a box of tissues in her lap. It looks like she's been crying, but she perks up and smiles when she sees me and Ricky.

"Hi, Sister Gwen," Ricky says politely.

Gwen gives a fake smile. "Hello, Ricky. Did you have a good game?"

"We lost, I'm afraid."

I interject, "Only because Coach Rogers doesn't have good sense. He won't start Ricky."

"Well, maybe next time. Ricky, you'd better be getting home. Your mother is going to be worried sick."

"Okay. See you tomorrow, Gia. Bye, Sister Gwen!"

Ricky walks out the door and I close it behind him. I turn around slowly because I can tell Gwen has started crying again. I wonder what it's all about.

"What's wrong, Mom?"

She laughs sadly. "Oh, nothing, Gia. I just think the Lord wants me to be single, that's all."

Oh boy. I should've seen this coming. It always happens like this. My mom starts dating a guy, they really seem to hit it off, and then she starts talking like she's gonna marry him. Next thing you know she's sitting somewhere crying her eyes out, eating chocolate, and talking about how much she can't stand her sister-in-law because she has it all.

"Elder LeRon?" I ask.

She nods. "He says he needs to focus on his ministry."

"Well, Mom, I don't think he was the man for you anyway. You are way too fly for him."

Gwen lets out a sad chuckle. "Go on to bed, Gia. You've got to be over at Mother Cranford's by nine."

"Okay. Good night."

"Good night, Gia."

"Oh, Mom, I forgot to ask you about this. A bunch of people are going to the movies on Sunday after church. Can I go?"

"I don't see why not. Good night, baby."

Okay, so I know that wasn't the whole truth. But can I really ask her about going out on a date right now? I mean, she's sitting up here crying over Elder LeRon, so I know she's not trying to hear about my almost love life.

When I get into the semiprivacy of my bedroom, I pull out my cell phone that's been buzzing on my hip since I got home from IHOP.

I have a text. From Romeo. It says, You was looking hawt tonight shorty

Woo-hoo! I was looking hawt!!! Is that an upgrade from hot? Is hawt just extra hot? I don't know and I don't care, because it's all good!

I take my shower and go to bed with a smile on my face, because I've got a date. A date with a football player.

Wow on top of wow.

★ 10 ★

"**B**aby, go and microwave me one of those Lean Cuisines and bring it to me with some sweet tea," Mother Cranford says in her sweet voice.

"Yes, Mother Cranford."

Okay, so this job is not so bad. Me and Ricky got here at nine in the morning and so far, I've cleaned the kitchen and bathroom, vacuumed the carpets, and Ricky has read Mother Cranford her daily devotional. I hope he doesn't think I'm sharing my money!

When the microwave oven beeps, I take Mother Cranford's sweet and sour chicken back into the living room and place it on the TV tray in front of her. "Here you go, Mother."

"Thank you, baby," she says with a smile.

I bet you all are wondering why we call her Mother Crabapple with all this sweet-talking and smiling going on. Well, don't let that fool you. When we were little, she would pinch somebody's leg with a quickness. Me, Ricky, and Hope would be standing in the sanctuary crying and none of our mamas knew why! It was Mother Crabapple and them hard bird talon fingernails.

Ricky is looking at the pictures on Mother Cranford's mantelpiece. He points to one that looks super ancient. In the picture is a young man in a military uniform and a banging young lady in a white sundress.

"Is this you, Mother Cranford?" Ricky asks.

She chuckles. "Yes, sir. That was in my heyday."

"You were a knockout, Mother!" Ricky exclaims.

Mother Cranford giggles. "Are you trying to make an old woman blush, boy?"

I step closer to the picture so that I can get a better look. Not only is Mother Cranford "wearing" that dress, but she's rocking a fierce afro with a flower tucked behind her ear. Who knew she was this fly?

I say, "Your hair is fresh to death, Mother."

"I'm assuming fresh to death is a good thing," Mother Cranford laughs. "You can wear your hair like that."

I shake my head. "I could never pull that look off. I need a relaxer and a wrap, but my mom won't let me."

"Well, sometimes you've got to work what you've got! Back when I was a girl, everybody had a press and curl."

My nose crinkles in disgust. "I hate those."

"I did too! I hated sitting still all them hours and getting burned on the neck! That's why I wore an Afro."

Ricky laughs. "Burned on the neck? Women go through a lot to look pretty."

"And boys don't appreciate any of it," I reply. I can hear Cherish singing "Unappreciated" on the soundtrack in my head.

Ricky smiles wistfully. "We appreciate it."

Grrr!!! I know he's referring to his fantasy in jeans and leather boots—Ms. Valerie.

"My husband sure appreciated me! Afro and all," Mother Cranford beams.

What! Mean old Mother Crabapple had a man? The surprises just keep on coming, don't they? I wonder if she pinched him when he got out of line.

"I didn't know you were married, Mother Cranford," I say sweetly.

"Yep. Twenty-five years before he went home to be with the Lord. The best twenty-five years of my life," she says with a hint of sadness in her voice. "He was my best friend."

Ricky gives Mother Cranford a hug and says, "I'm sure he was a good husband."

Mother Cranford smiles and nods. "Well, I guess y'all are done for today. Got any big plans for the weekend?"

Ricky replies, "I'll probably hang out with Kevin, but Gia's going to a party."

I cringe at the mention of Kevin. I don't need a visual of his face when I've been daydreaming about my date with Romeo.

Mother Cranford says, "Well, have fun, baby. You deserve it."

"Thank you, Mother," I reply.

A few minutes later, Valerie pulls up in the driveway

with a car full of girls. I look out Mother Cranford's big picture window and then back at Ricky.

I say, "You better act like you got some sense."

Ricky laughs and says, "Wow!"

We say good-bye to Mother Cranford and go out to the driveway. Valerie has gotten out and is leaning on the side of the car like she knew Ricky was here. Wait. Did she know he was going to be here? He's got a huge smile on his face.

"Hey, Hi-Stepper!" Valerie says to me.

"Hey, Valerie."

Valerie tosses her hair back and says, "You don't sound excited about your first Hi-Steppers' party."

I am excited about the party, but what I'm *not* excited about is how Ricky is drooling over the tight leather skirt that Valerie is wearing. All this ogling is getting real old.

Ricky says, "Hey, Valerie. You look nice today."

"Thank you, Rick," Valerie replies. She licks her slippery lips and continues, "I would invite you to the party, but no boys allowed."

"It's cool," Ricky says with a shrug. "I'm going to the rec to play ball with my boy Kev. See y'all later."

Valerie grabs Ricky's arm as he tries to walk away and he looks like he's about to have a serious meltdown. Dang! All she did was touch his arm.

"Wait a minute, Rick," Valerie says. "A little birdie told me that Romeo and Gia are going to the movies tomorrow. Why don't we make it a double date?"

Okay, first of all, I should've known that Stupid Is and Stupid Does were going to tell Valerie about my date. That was just plain inevitable. But for real though, who invited Valerie to kick it with me and my new boo? And I most definitely don't want Ricky there, 'cause he will spend the entire time blocking. Me no likee.

But Ricky obviously likes the idea. He says, "Cool! We can all meet up at the mall. That'll give me and Gia time to change out of our church clothes."

Valerie replies, "You know what? I was thinking of visiting your church tomorrow anyway."

Ricky hugs Valerie. "You should! You'll really enjoy the service."

Okay, now I'm going to have to ask the Lord for forgiveness, because am I not supposed to be happy when someone wants to come to church? Truth is, I'm not unhappy, but I'm definitely not as excited as Mr. Hugs-a-lot Ricky.

As Ricky jogs down the driveway and up the street, Valerie licks her lips and smiles. "He is too fine."

She's going to end up with a rash on her mouth doing all that lip licking. I mean, seriously, how moist do one's lips really need to be? What? I'm not hating. I'm just saying. There is a difference.

I ask, "Don't you think that's kind of blasphemous— going to church just to hook up with a boy?"

"Who said that was the *only* reason? I like church! My mom takes me twice a year," Valerie replies with a giggle.

I just roll my eyes and get into the backseat of Valerie's Honda Civic. There are two seniors in the car too, and they don't even speak to me. Now, ask me if I care.

"So, Gia," Valerie says, "I got you a present. Portia, hand her the bag."

Portia hands me a bag from the beauty supply store. I open it and look inside. There is a long brown ponytail with blond streaks, and other hair products. There's also a bunch of lipsticks, mascaras and other makeup.

Valerie says, "Look, Gia, Romeo asked you out because you're a Hi-Stepper and he thinks you have potential."

"I'm not wearing all this stuff," I reply with much attitude.

"Don't you want to make the A squad too?" Valerie asks. "This isn't just about Romeo, you know."

Man, I want to wear those little white boots so badly, I can taste it. "Okay, Valerie, I'll do the ponytail, but we've got to chill on the makeup. My mother isn't on that."

Valerie laughs. "Girl, you don't know how to wipe it off before you get home?"

I laugh too, but not because what Valerie says is funny. I'm laughing because she doesn't know Sister Gwen. Old girl be pulling out moves from the old kung fu movies. I think one time I saw her glide through the air right before she went upside my head. She looked just like Jet Li's auntie. I kid you not.

"Look, just give it a try," Valerie says. "If you don't like it, then you don't have to wear it."

We pull up to Valerie's house, where several of the Hi-Steppers, including Hope, are gathered on the porch. Hope is standing off to the side with her arms crossed, and she has a serious frown on her face. I wonder what's got her twisted.

"It's about time y'all got here!" Kelani squeals.

Everyone goes inside and starts on the potato chips, pop,

and freshly delivered pizza. I don't hear anyone asking about the carb counts tonight. I guess that means even Hi-Steppers do goodie binges.

While everyone is grubbing on the junk food, Valerie says, "Don't think y'all can eat like this all the time. You greedy heifers better still be fitting into those skirts next week."

"You don't have to worry about that, Gia," Jewel says. "I guess you can eat all you want."

Everyone bursts into laughter. Okay, yeah, they're gonna have to simmer down with all these skinny Gia jokes. I'm not laughing because they are not funny. I almost respond, but then I figure that it's not even worth it. I'm gonna keep my cool, especially since they had that messy performance on Friday.

After we all finish eating, Valerie announces, "Okay, everybody, it's makeover time."

Everyone in the room turns and looks at me, like I'm the obvious choice. Why isn't anybody looking at the glitter twins? They temporarily blinded me when they stepped into the sun.

"What are y'all looking at me for?" I ask.

Valerie answers, "Come on, Gia, you already know what it is."

Jewel and Portia each grab one of my arms and lead me to Valerie's oversized bathroom. Valerie pops the rubber band out of my afro puff.

"Hey!" I shout. "That hurt! This afro is attached to a tender head."

Valerie laughs. "Step one. Wash and condition this bush."

They wash my hair with something that smells a lot better than the stuff me and Gwen use. But I suppose Valerie doesn't get her hair supplies from the dollar store. My scalp is still tingling when they push me down in a chair at Valerie's little vanity table.

Portia attacks my head with gel and a hairbrush. I scream, "Ow! That hurts!"

"Just think of how Romeo's gonna look at you on your date tomorrow," Valerie encourages.

Hope's mouth drops open. "Does Auntie Gwen know you're going on a date with a football player?"

Valerie shoots her an evil look. "No, and she better not find out from you."

Hope drops her head submissively, but seriously, I don't think I'm safe from her hateration. Hope would just love the opportunity to get me in trouble. She's been doing that since we were little, so it's nothing new.

"Okay, close your eyes," Jewel says while holding a miniature razor in her hand.

Uh-uh. I don't even think so. I put up both hands to block her from coming any closer. "Where do you think you're going with that blade?"

Valerie takes my hands and places them in my lap. "That unibrow has got to go, sweetheart."

I'm afraid. I'm *very* afraid.

"Do you know what you're doing?" I ask with a little tremble in my voice.

"Yes, Gia. I do everyone's eyebrows. I usually charge five bucks, but since this is an intervention, I'm doing it for free."

I squeeze my eyes shut and Jewel commences to scrap-

ing. The noise has me imagining that I might end up looking like Whoopi Goldberg. I mean, she's a proud sista
and all, but the woman gave up on eyebrows years ago. I
happen to like my eyebrows.

After a few minutes Jewel's done, and if I can judge by
everyone's oohs and ahs, it must be looking right. I feel
my heartbeat go back to its normal pace.

"I need a mirror!" I say, anxiously wanting to see what
my face looks like.

Valerie shakes her head. "Nope. Not until we're done.
We want to do a big reveal!"

A big reveal? Wow. It is really not that serious, people.

Portia snatches my hair into the tightest ponytail ever.
I know that I'm looking like one of Kimora Lee Simmons's
little quarter Asian babies right about now. Portia snaps
the fake hair on top of my own with a scary quickness.

Finally, Valerie hits me up with some glitter eye shadow,
mascara, and eyeliner. Then she slicks some of the shini-
est lip gloss I've ever seen on my lips. When she's done,
Valerie steps back and looks at her masterpiece.

"Ooo-OOO! You lookin' fierce, girlfriend!"

Someone hands me a mirror, and even though I'm fear-
ful, I put it up to my face. Next, I feel my jaw drop open.
I cannot believe what I'm seeing.

No, seriously, I don't believe it.

I look like Alicia Keys's baby sister. Okay, Alica Keys's
skinny little sister. But still! I can't stop grinning at my reflection.

Then it hits me. Gwen is gonna freak out.

After everyone congratulates me—well, everyone minus
Hope—we go downstairs to the family room to watch scary

movies. I hate scary movies, but I go along with everyone else. I can just close my eyes during the bloody parts.

As we all sit down, Hope whispers in my ear, "You know Auntie Gwen isn't going to let you out the house looking like that, right?"

"What's wrong, Hope?" I whisper back. "Are you just mad because for once you're not the center of attention?"

"I could care less," Hope replies with a toss of her hair.

I toss my brand new ponytail right back. "That's 'I *couldn't* care less.'"

"You're such a nerd."

"Romeo doesn't think so."

Hope spins on one heel. "Do you think he really likes you? Valerie probably put him up to it, or maybe he thinks you'll be stupid enough to give him some."

It feels like Hope just hit me with a brick. "Why would he think that?"

Hope laughs. "Busted girls are usually easy."

I guess she feels like she accomplished something, because she struts over to the couch and sits down between Jewel and Kelani with a satisfied smile on her face. Could she be right, though? I don't know what would be worse, Valerie putting him up to a date with me or him thinking I'm easy.

But we all know she isn't right about me being *busted*. That's not even worth discussing.

Since all of the seats are taken, I sit down on the carpeted floor next to Portia. She actually smiles at me and hands me a couch pillow. Is this all I needed to be popular? A fake ponytail and some lip gloss? Wow.

Valerie stands in front of the television. "Okay, y'all,

before I turn on the movie, I have a Hi-Steppers announcement to make."

Everyone starts murmuring, and Valerie puts a hand up. "Quiet please. We know that we had a horrible, horrible performance on Friday."

A few people look at Hope. Valerie continues, "I don't know why y'all looking at Hope. One person's mistake shouldn't be able to mess up half the line. Every single last one of y'all have messed up before."

Hope looks a little bit relieved. But not much.

"But in light of the ridiculous foolishness that was the Hi-Steppers' line on Friday, I'm making some changes to our lineup."

Every single Hi-Stepper gasps. Except me, of course. I didn't mess up the line.

Valerie then drops the bomb. "Gia, I'm upgrading you to the A squad."

No one congratulates me. I guess they're waiting to see who's getting dropped to the B squad, although it should be obvious.

"Hope," Valerie says sweetly, "I'm sorry, but for now you're going to have to chill on the B squad. I'm sure you'll get to move up next year since we've got a few Hi-Steppers graduating."

The two giggle heifers chuckle under their breath. Wow, aren't they good friends? Hope bursts into tears, and I try to comfort her by touching her hand. She shoves me away and runs out to the porch bawling.

There's an uncomfortable silence in the room, and everyone looks at Valerie to tell us what to do next.

Valerie holds up a DVD. "Y'all ready for *Aliens*?"

This is too harsh. Hope is in the other room crying and they're just going to watch a movie like it's all good. I can't let it go down like that, so as much as I hate to do it, I get up and go outside on the porch with Hope.

Her back is to mine, but I ask her in a whisper, "Are you okay?"

"Why do you care?" she asks. "You got what you wanted. You're on the A squad now."

"Well, I didn't want you to get hurt, that's for sure."

She turns to face me with tears in her eyes. "I wouldn't have cared if it was you. I didn't care when you got put on the B squad to begin with. I wouldn't have cared if you didn't make the team at all."

"Wow . . . Okay then. I'm going back in the house. And you can go back to crying if you want." My words don't have any emotion attached to them because I don't know how to feel. I'm trying to help her and she's deliberately hurting my feelings.

"You know what else?" Hope asks. "I wish you weren't my cousin. You're so embarrassing with your stupid-looking clothes and nappy hair. I wish you would just disappear."

Tears sting my eyes, but I'm not going to let Hope see them fall. I spin quickly on one heel and walk back into the house. Sadly, I take a seat next to Valerie on the floor.

Valerie whispers to me, "Don't worry. She'll get over it."

I nod in agreement because I know that Hope will get over it. She's just going to have to get over it without me, because I give up. If she doesn't want me for a cousin, then she's not going to have me.

* * *

While everyone's watching the movie and Hope's still outside, I sneak into the bathroom to call Ricky. I hate to admit this, but an hour has gone by and I'm still on the verge of tears.

"Hey, Gia. What's up? Aren't you over Valerie's house?" Ricky asks.

"Y-yes," I reply as the tears unwillingly start to fall.

Ricky says, "What's the matter? Are you crying? Do you need me to come over there?"

So I tell Ricky all about Hope getting sent to the B squad and about how she said all of those mean and hurtful things to me. The more I talk, the harder I cry, because it all sounds so awful.

"Wow," Ricky says after I'm done. "I can't believe she said all of that to you."

"Well, she did."

"I don't think she means any of it. She's just angry and needed to lash out at someone. I know she didn't mean it."

I'm glad Ricky is convinced, because I'm definitely not. I don't know whether Hope meant what she said or not. And as far as her lashing out at me, well a sista can only take so much.

"What is this all about?" Gwen asks after looking me up and down.

I didn't want to come home from Valerie's house before church because I was sure that Gwen was gonna trip. But Valerie's mother took everyone home so that she could get some peace and quiet. Valerie promised to show up at church, but I'm definitely not holding my breath.

Anyway, Gwen is straight staring me down. She narrows her eyes, places one hand on her hip and waits for an explanation.

I take a deep breath and answer her question with a question. "What's all what about?"

"Gia, don't get hurt this morning. This is the Lord's day."

I slowly touch my ponytail. "Oh. You mean this?"

"Yes. When did you start wearing hair weave?"

She sounds irritated, and this makes me afraid. Very

afraid. I take two steps back until I'm out of her arm's reach. Then I reply, "I thought I'd try something new."

"Let me rephrase my question," she says as she takes two steps in my direction. "When did I give you permission to put fake hair on top of your head or take a razor blade to your eyebrows?"

"It's just a ponytail, and my eyebrows looked crazy, Mom."

Gwen sighs and flares her nostrils. I close my eyes tightly and brace myself for the pain. Then she says, "Well . . . I guess it's all right."

"What?" Did my ears hear correctly or have I already gone home to be with Jesus?

"You are growing up, I guess. It's cute. But don't even think about wearing any makeup. That's where I draw the line."

Since she's okay with this, maybe the Lord has opened her eyes to some other things. "So are you saying I can get a relaxer too?"

"Don't test me, girl. Go on and get in the car so we can make it to church on time. Elder LeRon is opening the service."

Oh, brother. She's back on Elder LeRon again. Two days ago, that was a done deal. My mom stays trying to convince a man to get with her. I wish she would just be happy being single. I mean, am I not enough?

"I thought he wasn't feeling you."

"Girl, I never said that. I said he was focusing on his ministry."

"Okay . . ."

"So, I talked to God about it, and I still feel in my spirit that he's the man for me. I just have to be faithful."

Wow. I don't even know what to say to this. Gwen is a great mom, but she just has this thing going on when it comes to men. Sometimes, I think that all she cares about in life is finding a man and getting him to marry her.

"Well, what are you waiting on, Gia? You and your hair can go get in the car. I'm right behind you."

As we ride down our street, I say, "Mom, can I ask you a question?"

"Sure, baby. Ask away."

"Why does Hope hate me so much?"

Gwen lets out a long sigh. "I don't think she hates you, Gia. She's just having growing pains."

"Why does everyone keep giving her excuses?" I ask angrily. "I'm always trying to be nice to her and have her back and she just treats me like dirt."

"I know it's not fair, but Hope is trying to figure out who she is. It's tough being the pastor's daughter."

Are you kidding me? What's tough about that? Everyone in the church ignores all of the mean stuff that she does and they're always trying to be her friend. Her parents have money and they give her any and everything that she wants. What's so hard about that?

Gwen says, "I see you over there and I know what you're thinking. I was a pastor's daughter, Gia, so I understand what Hope is going through."

"She has everything, Mom. What could she possibly be going through?"

"Well, first of all, everything she does affects her father. If she cuts up in church, they blame him. If she gets caught out acting fast, people start asking how he can run the church if he can't run his own household. Everyone might love the pastor's family, but they also feel free to judge them whenever they feel like it. It's hard to be under everyone's microscope."

I ask, "Is that why you were out of control when you were a teenager?"

"I wasn't out of control," Gwen says. "I was stupid and thought that no one knew anything but me. I thought I was in love with your father."

She did? Wow. We never talk about my mom as a teenager and we certainly never talk about my dad.

"What was he like?" I ask.

"Your daddy? Well, he was really handsome, but he was a thug. He and his friends would just visit our church looking for girls to hook up with."

I scrunch my eyebrows and frown. "So why did you hook up with him?"

"Because everyone, including my daddy, told me not to. I was sick of being told what I could and could not do."

I can definitely relate to this. But I don't understand my mom. If she felt that way when she was my age, then why does she put all these crazy rules on me?

Gwen continues. "After I got pregnant with you, I realized that everyone was just trying to protect me. I felt bad, because I ended up hurting everyone around me. They wanted Grandpa Stokes to step down as pastor."

I ask in a quiet voice, "Do you wish you never had me?"

"Of course not! You are the reason I keep going every day."

"But you don't regret any of it?"

My mother sighs and says, "I missed my prom, didn't get to go away for school, and had to get my diploma in the mail over the summer. My father refused to let me cross the stage with a big stomach."

My mother has been through a lot, I see. I guess I kind of understand now why she's so hard on me. But I know that I'm not going to repeat her mistakes. I wish she had more faith in me.

Gwen and I walk into the sanctuary just as the youth praise team takes the stage. Ricky is leading a song and he sounds good. He's even got some of the church mothers standing on their feet and rocking back and forth.

Of course, the girls sitting in the young people's row are standing up too. They are the ones who are only here because their parents made them show up. Usually, I ignore them, but today, the young people have a visitor— Valerie.

I didn't think she'd actually show up, much less on time. But there she is in a too short skirt, clapping her hands together and hollering for Ricky when she should be hollering for Jesus. I know that the Lord cannot possibly be pleased, so where is the lightning when I need it?

Gwen looks over at Valerie and whispers to me as we sit down in a pew, "Isn't that your friend from school?"

"That's Valerie, the one who had the sleepover."

I don't know if I want to call her my friend yet, because she hasn't really done anything for me that didn't benefit her. She put me on the A squad of the Hi-Steppers because Hope was making them look stupid. She gave me a makeover so that I don't embarrass the other Hi-Steppers with my signature look.

Yes. Tweety and afro puffs are a signature look. That's real talk.

But back to Valerie. I don't really have any evidence that she's my friend yet. A friend doesn't throw you under the bus.

Hope thought Valerie was *her* friend, but now she's got tire tracks on her back.

Pastor preaches a message about how we should love our neighbors and our enemies. He talks about how Jesus even prayed for people who hated him. I guess that means I should pray for Hope.

But can I wait until next week? Because I'm so not feeling her today. Especially since she's mean-mugging me from across the sanctuary. She's got a smirk on her face that tells me she's up to no good.

After service, Hope runs up to my mother and gives her a hug. "Hey, Auntie Gwen!"

Now I know something is up.

Gwen smiles at Hope and says, "Well, what is the occasion that I get a hug?"

"I just thought we should celebrate!" Hope is smiling but she looks at me with pure evil in her eyes.

"What are we celebrating?"

Hope claps her hands together like she's truly happy. "Gia's first date!"

Ooh, I could really slap the taste out of her mouth right now. If I didn't know it before, I know it now—Hope hates me. She truly, truly hates me if she would cause me to become a victim of violence.

Gwen spins on her heel and stands nose to nose with me. "Gia's first what?"

"Oh, she didn't tell you? She's got a date with a player on the football team. They're going to the movies right after church."

Gwen's entire face turns a crazy shade of red. I can't think of anything to say that will fix this. I just hope I can get away before she snatches this ponytail off my head.

At this very moment, Valerie walks up. "Hope, what are you talking about? A bunch of us do plan to go to the movies after church. But nobody's going on a date. Rick is going too."

Gwen looks Valerie up and down, but doesn't stop frowning. "Who is Rick?"

"She means Ricky, Mom," I explain.

Valerie continues, "I just think that Hope is upset she wasn't invited."

"Well, I don't believe in that," Gwen says. "If you invite Gia, then you need to invite Hope. They are cousins."

Oh no! Gwen just invited Hope on my date. And she's standing there grinning at the mess she's caused. I'm going to get her for this.

"You're right, Ms. Stokes," Valerie says, and then she looks at Hope with the pure evil eye. "Do you want to go to the movies with us, Hope?"

Hope replies, "Sure! I'd love to go!"

"Well, there it is," Gwen says with a satisfied tone in her voice. "Y'all go and have fun."

Valerie and Hope head out to the parking lot, both glaring at one another. But I've got a small smile on my face, because I think that Valerie just got my back. She did, right? Gwen was about to do me bodily harm, and Valerie swooped right on in with an alibi.

Just when I'm about to exit the church too, Gwen grabs my arm and lets me know that I'm not home free. She hisses in my ear, "Listen, Ms. Thang. If you think you can fool me, you better think again. Don't be foolish. If I catch you hugged up with some boy, I will send you straight to your final resting place. Do you hear me?"

"Yes."

"Yes, what?"

I blink back tears as Gwen's acrylic nails dig into my arm. "Yes, ma'am."

Finally she releases my arm and lets the blood flow freely. "Now go on and go to the movies. And you better watch yourself, because you don't know where I'll turn up."

Talk about fear tactics. Gwen is on some other stuff, for real. She's trying to take all the fun out of this. I mean, seriously, can you imagine her jumping from behind a row of seats at the movies? Snatching off her church hat and going upside my head with it? Dang, that would not be a good look. It would be downright embarrassing.

So, I walk out to the parking lot too, no longer excited about all this . . . only hoping to survive the afternoon. Hope has her head tossed back, mid-giggle, and Valerie is mean-mugging her the whole time.

Hope asks, "So where am I sitting in your car, Val? The front or the back?"

"Rick will be riding shotgun. You can take your hating behind to the backseat," Valerie replies. "You better be glad you aren't riding in the trunk."

"It's cool, Valerie," I say, trying to halt any arguments.

It's already bad enough that I've got to look at Hope all day.

Running out of the church with Kevin by his side, Ricky asks, "So, are we about to go now?"

"We sure are!" Valerie replies with a smile. "I thought you were about to stand me up."

Ricky smiles slowly (and looking right fine). "Never that."

I have never seen Ricky smile at anyone like that. He looks like a cross between Nelly and Chris Brown when he does that. Wait, who am I going on a date with again? That's right . . . Romeo . . . six-feet tall, Bow Wow look-alike. Right. Thanks for reminding me.

I see Kevin try to make eye contact with me, so I quickly scramble into the backseat of Valerie's Honda Civic. For some reason, I don't want to tell him about my date. I guess it'll make him feel bad, and guilt is not my favorite feeling.

Kevin, though, doesn't plan to let me off the hook. He thrusts his pimply face into the backseat window and says, "Praise the Lord, Gia!"

Since I don't want him to p-p-praise me again, I just do the necessary. "Praise the Lord, boy! Now, fall back."

"Where are you guys going? Can I come with?" he asks, ignoring all of my obvious meanness.

"Ugh! Noneya biznass and no!"

Hope laughs. "Hey, Kevin, your little girlfriend here is playing you. We're on our way to her very first date."

"Well, why are you going then, Hope?" Kevin asks, not wanting to believe. "Is it some kind of group date?"

Ricky pats Kevin on the back. "You can come, Kev! Valerie's got room."

Simultaneously, Valerie and I shout, "NO!"

"Why not? Kev is cool!" Ricky says.

Since no one speaks up quickly enough, Kevin opens the door and smashes me into a hater sandwich between him and Hope. I can't believe this. Can a sista get a date up in here? This must be direct punishment from the Lord for lying to Gwen.

Hope and Kevin spend the entire ride to the mall chatting about nothing. She's more than jolly and he keeps spitting over my chest to answer her questions.

So, we pull up to the mall and Romeo is standing out front. Well, he's not really standing, 'cause he's way too fresh to be standing. Dude is just posted up in front of the mall, looking like he couldn't care less about being there.

Too, too hot.

When our little ragtag crew finally gets to the front of the mall, Romeo places one hand over his mouth and says, "Dang, baby girl! You looking right!"

"Thank you, Romeo," I reply, trying not to turn red.

He looks me up and down and keeps the compliments coming. "I mean, your hair is fresh and your gear is fresh to death! You must be really digging Romeo. Am I right?"

I take a deep gulp. I like this guy, I think, but I'm not feeling him referring to himself in the third person. Ugh! Gia is not pleased.

I respond, "I don't know yet. We'll see."

Valerie laughs. "That's right, boo. He ain't got you open like that! Ooo-OOO!"

She gives me a high-five and a proud smile. Hope is real salty. Oh well. That's what she gets for hating.

Romeo says, "All right. I see you. But what's up with all the company? I thought this was a double date."

"Looks like it's a triple," Valerie says with a chuckle. "Hope wanted to bring her little man too, so we couldn't leave her out. Hi-Steppers don't play one another."

Hope rolls her eyes and intelligently decides not to respond. Kevin decides to perform his gentlemanly duties and grabs Hope's elbow, pulling her over the curb. She snatches her arm away and storms into the mall.

Valerie laughs out loud. "That's right, Kevin. Get your boo!"

Like I said . . . that's what she gets for hating.

We get up to the window to pay for our tickets, and Romeo says, "I got you, boo."

Well, all right. He just might have made up for all of that third-person nonsense with this. Now, all he has to do is get me some refreshments. What? I love me some popcorn and Goobers, why you playing?

So, why is Hope looking crazy because she doesn't have any money? She was so busy with her little hater scheme that she forgot to get money from her dad. I'm certainly not footing the bill for her. For all I care she can stand out in the mall.

"I'll pay for you," Kevin volunteers.

Valerie and I both burst out in laughter. Hope looks like she wants to cry, but she says, "Okay, Kevin, but I'm not sitting next to you."

"That's not cool, Hope," Ricky says with a frown. "You should be thanking him."

Valerie adds, "I know, right! Some people are so ungrateful. Kevin is just being a gentleman helping an ungrateful damsel in distress."

I could add my own two cents, but for some crazy reason, I feel sorry for Hope. Yeah, I know. I shouldn't have any sympathy for her, as horrible as she's been toward me. It's just that her whole plan backfired on her and now it's not even funny anymore. I wouldn't want to be stuck dealing with moist-palms Kevin for an entire two hours.

But . . . I don't feel bad enough to speak up for her. She did just trip on me in a major way.

We walk into an almost empty theater. I guess nobody wanted to see *My Mama's Family Reunion* on a Sunday afternoon. Whatev. I didn't come here for the movie. I came for the company.

Did I tell y'all how good Romeo smells? Oh my goodness. I don't know what kind of cologne he's wearing, but I'm gonna need to find out so I can spray it on my pillow and smell him twenty-four/seven.

Romeo is pulling me away from everyone else, so that we can have a seat off in the corner. Immediately, an image of a karate-chopping Gwen floats through my brain. Plus, I'm not stupid. I know what's supposed to happen once the lights go down in the theater.

"Umm . . . can we sit with everyone else?" I ask.

Romeo lets out a long sigh. "Yeah, it's cool."

I know he doesn't have the audacity to sound irritated! I mean, what did he think was going down during this flick? He better simmer his hormones on down.

I end up sitting between Romeo and Valerie with Ricky on the end. Hope and Kevin sit one row in front of us, with an empty seat between them.

Valerie whispers to Hope, "Aren't you going to sit next to your date?"

"Shut up, Valerie," she hisses.

Valerie laughs. "Shut up? You must not be trying to get that spot back on the A squad. And don't forget I'm the one who brought you up here. Don't make me leave you."

Hope instantly starts backtracking. "I do want my spot back, but I'm not going to let you embarrass me."

"That's enough, Valerie," I say with a smirk. "I'm not giving up my spot anyway."

Hope rolls her eyes and knocks Kevin's hand away when he tries to offer some popcorn.

We're here super early, so I'm tripping trying to think of conversation to get us through the little advertisements they show on the movie screen. Romeo doesn't seem to be much of a talker as he's slumped real low in his seat, still wearing his sunglasses. I'm not even going to mention that there's not one hint of sunlight in here; neither was there outside. All we're seeing on this October day is cloudy and extra cloudy.

Trying to break the silence, I ask Romeo, "So, do you think Coach Rogers is gonna start Ricky at all this season?"

Romeo laughs. "Naw. Not while he's trying to get his son a scholarship."

"Just drop it, Gia. I'm not stressing over it," Ricky says, but clearly he is stressing over it, because he sounds too irritated.

Valerie interjects, "Well, you *should* be stressing over it. How you gonna be my dude sitting on the bench?"

Ricky blinks his big old eyes, way too many times. Is he for real? Then he comes with this mess, "You want me to be your dude?"

"Maybe . . ." Valerie says like she's all undecided.

I'm trying not to get angry, because I don't want *my* little dude over here to get jealous. But I'm tripping on this Valerie and Ricky stuff. Not because I want him, but because I know she's going to play him. It's inevitable. I mean, why do the lions have to attack the zebras on the Discovery channel? It's what they do!

The chick is a straight predator.

And then he'll come crying to me. Hmm . . . Perhaps this isn't such a bad thing. Okay, let me stop. I'm supposed to be focusing on Romeo.

Finally, the lights dim completely and the movie starts. I'm about half done with my popcorn and starting in on my chocolate. Romeo removes his sunglasses, sits up in his seat and smiles at me. I feel butterflies, moths, and dragonflies buzzing all over my stomach. I have to look away because his gaze is way too intense. Entirely too much eye contact for me.

Valerie whispers in my ear, "He's really feeling you, girl. I can tell."

I don't respond because Romeo has shifted in his seat and placed his arm on the armrest that I'm already using. As our arms and shoulders touch lightly, I feel my breath nearly stop, and my stomach flip-flops.

I don't think I'm ready for all this.

But then, Romeo goes and makes it worse, by whispering to me with his hot, steamy breath, "Am I gonna get a kiss, shorty?"

How can I be excited and irritated at exactly the same moment?

Because first and foremost, dude has paid for a movie

ticket and some snacks and he's trying to push up on the lips? Umm . . . not so fast, son! These lips are virgin lips, and I need him to be my *boyfriend* before this is even a discussion.

But I'm still excited, though . . . because he wants to kiss me! Whoa!

I reply, "I'm not sure if you've earned a kiss yet, Romeo."

"Romeo has earned a kiss by being Romeo," he says with a laugh. "But I see you playing hard to get. Romeo likes a chase, so it's all good."

Ricky glances down at us and rolls his eyes. He's not feeling all the Romeo this and Romeo that. Neither am I really, but did I tell you that Romeo's lips look plump and soft like two little pillows?

Okay, I've got to pull myself together. Me tripping on this guy is the opposite of my style. But something in me is ignoring all common sense. I need a distraction . . . for real, for real.

Thank God for the utter foolishness that is Kevin!

He's trying to share his popcorn with Hope and she's ignoring him. So, he scoots over into the empty seat that is between them. He's leaning over the armrest grinning at her. I'm just too through with him! He's supposed to be in love with me and he's moved right on to Hope. He's got some nerve.

Hope growls at him, "Fall back, Kevin."

"I was just seeing if you wanted some p-p-popcorn!" Yes, he did spray the salty snack with his secret saliva sauce.

"I don't want none of your popcorn, Kevin! Can you just get back to your seat?" Hope is leaning as far away from Kevin as possible.

For the first time ever, Kevin looks salty! He stands up, blocking everybody's view, and shouts, "You don't have the right to treat me like this, Hope. I'm telling your father."

"Tell him!" Hope says with a laugh. "Do you think he'll listen to me or you? Get real, Kevin, and take a seat. You're blocking the movie screen."

Kevin stands there holding that box of popcorn in one hand and balling his other hand into a fist. His face is red, and his eyebrows are knotted into a crazy frown. For a brief second, I think he's about to swing on Hope. As ignorant as she is, neither Ricky nor I will sit up here and watch her get beat down.

Ricky tries to calm him down. "Kev, man, it's cool. Chill."

"It is not cool," Kevin says extra loud, disturbing the other five people in this theater trying to watch the movie. "She's been dogging me out since we got here, for no reason! And she's supposed to be the pastor's daughter!"

"What does that have to do with anything?" Valerie asks. Clearly she's not up on church politics.

Hope laughs. "Boy, sit down! I don't have to be nice to you."

Kevin's eyes get as big as two saucers and behind his glasses they look even bigger. He makes some kind of growling battle cry and then does the most hilarious thing I've ever seen in person. He takes that super-sized box of hot, salty, buttery popcorn and pours it right on Hope's head.

Hope screams. "KEVIN! What is WRONG with you?"

We, of course, are cracking up. That's what she gets for being a witch to Kevin when he was just trying to be nice to her. Even Romeo, who seemed irritated by the whole scenario, is holding his stomach from laughing so hard. Kevin's chest is heaving up and down, but he seems to feel better.

Ricky steps out of his seat and into Kevin and Hope's row. Then he puts his arm around Kevin's shoulders. "Come on, Kev. Let's go outside so you can cool off."

Kevin looks ready to object, but for some reason he changes his mind and goes with Ricky. Valerie looks really heated that her date is going off to calm Kevin down.

Hope stands to her feet and brushes most of the popcorn from her clothes. But she misses all of the kernels that are in her hair and stuck to her neck.

Valerie laughs out loud. "You look a mess, girl," she says.

Hope narrows her eyes. "Isn't one of you going to help me?"

Valerie looks at me and Romeo and sighs. "I guess since this is Gia's first date and all, I'll help your lame self. Come on, let's go into the bathroom."

Valerie then trudges up the aisle. Hope is not far behind and she's leaving a popcorn trail behind her. I giggle to my-self—a little from the funny but mostly from the fact that Romeo and I are finally alone. Yeah, it's a nervous giggle.

"I'm your first date?" Romeo asks as if he didn't know.

"Yeah. I guess so."

Romeo smiles and asks, "So, how many other firsts do you want Romeo to be?"

Good question. But on the real, I haven't even really thought past the whole first date thing. Matter of fact, the first date is enough for me right now. I'm not trying to even think about anything like my first boyfriend, first kiss or first— See I can't even say it.

When I don't answer Romeo's question, he asks another

one. "Don't you want Romeo to be your first teenage love affair?"

I'm gonna let him slide on the simple fact that I love me some Alicia Keys and he can quote her songs all day and all night and I won't get mad. But, if he keeps referring to himself in the third person, I might be tossing a box of popcorn myself.

"I don't know, Romeo," I reply. "I'm just in chill mode right now."

"All right, shorty, I'm cool with that. But having all these extra haters around is not the business. I need some one-on-one time, you know what I mean?"

I feel myself suck a sharp breath through my nose. He wants alone time? As in me and him and his hormones? Me don't know if me likee.

"You want to go out? Just the two of us?"

Romeo nods. "Yep. How about next Saturday night? We can go see the late show over at Mentor Mall."

"Mentor Mall? That's on the other side of town! I'd never be able to make it back in time for curfew."

Romeo smiles and takes my face in his hands. "You'll figure something out."

Before I can answer, Ricky and Kevin come back into the theater and both sit down for the end of the movie. Ricky plops down in the seat next to me. Romeo looks a little stressed, but he doesn't say anything.

"So much for your first date," Ricky whispers.

Whatever! I'm not even going to count this haterfest as my first date. My big day is coming up next Saturday. All I have to do now is think of a plan.

★ 12 ★

I can't believe I'm actually doing this. I'm asking Valerie
for help.

If I'm going to come up with a plan to see Romeo next
Saturday night, it needs to be flawless. But, on the real, I
don't have too much practice with the whole deceiving
my mama thing. And if Gwen finds out about me creeping, I may never date again. Ever.

Shoot, I may never walk again.

So, I'm standing here at Valerie's locker waiting for
her. School is already out, and I'm feeling real nice because not only is Romeo feeling me (his homeboy gave
me a note from him during fourth period) but I aced my
history test. I got a big fat one hundred percent. Essay questions are my thing and this test was full of them.

Here comes Valerie sashaying herself down the hall.
Today she's got curls instead of her straight do. It's pinned

over to one side and cascading over one of her shoulders. Who does she think she is, J.Lo's baby cousin?

I'm glad she's alone, because I don't want any of her little followers all up in my business, especially the bedazzled twins, Jewel and Kelani. And definitely, positively not Hater Hope. This mission is top secret.

"What's up, Hi-Stepper?" Valerie asks. "Shouldn't you be getting dressed for practice?"

I nod. "Yes, but I need a favor."

"What kind of favor?" Valerie tilts her head to one side and narrows her eyes like she's trying to read my mind.

I reply, "Well . . . Romeo asked me out on another date."

She gives me a high-five. "I knew he was feeling you! So do you need to borrow an outfit or something?"

I wish it was something that simple. "Umm . . . no. I kind of need for you to say I'm spending the night over your house on Saturday. . . ."

"What?" Valerie asks with a giggle. "You want me to cover for you? I thought you church kids didn't lie."

"Well, it won't exactly be a lie. I'll come to your house and you and I will go out to Mentor Mall."

"Mentor Mall? Why y'all going all the way out there?"

I shrug my shoulders. "I don't know. That's where Romeo wants to go."

"Hmm . . . the only thing is, I've got a date on Saturday myself."

I lift one of my eyebrows suspiciously. "That's funny. Ricky didn't mention it."

Valerie swings her locker open and says casually, "That's because Rick doesn't know about it. I'm going out with Brad."

I take a deep breath. I want to start tripping hard. How is she playing my boy like that? And then having the audacity to tell me? If I didn't need her right about now, we'd probably already be brawling.

And how she gonna play Ricky for Brad? Or should I say Bradley? He's super uptight and is always talking about how he's going to an Ivy League school. He stays looking crazy in those pseudo-preppy cardigan sweaters that he buys at Target. Boo to Bradley!

I guess she can sense my anger because she says, "Before you start blowing up, Gia, Rick and I are not exclusive yet. When he wants me to not see anyone else, he'll let me know."

"Does *he* know you're not exclusive?" I ask. "Because I don't see him trying to holla at anyone else."

Valerie bursts into laughter. "Well, of course he's not dating anyone else! How can he upgrade me?"

Why'd she go and say that? Now, I'm going to have Beyoncé and Jay-Z singing in my head for the rest of the day.

I say, "I don't know, Valerie. It seems kind of grimy. Ricky is too nice for all that. And did you forget that he's my best friend?"

"Yeah, yeah, yeah. I know he used to be your best friend. But you're a Hi-Stepper now."

"And . . ."

"And that means we've got each other's back," Valerie explains. "Just like I'm about to have your back."

I fold my arms and gaze at Valerie suspiciously. "How are you going to do that?"

"Well, if you don't mention this conversation to Ricky,

I will reschedule my date with Brad and hook up a miniature sleepover."

Of course, I can't answer right away. She's asking me to help her scheme on my best friend. I know he'd never do that to me.

But . . . would he understand how important this date is with Romeo? Nobody has ever been checking for me except Kevin. Nobody. I mean I've been right under Ricky's nose all this time and he's never even looked twice at me.

If Romeo asks me to be his girl, it'll be on and popping for real. Nobody will call me lame for getting straight A's, nobody will call me skinny, and nobody will clown my clothes. I need this. I need this so much.

If I were Ricky, I would understand.

"Okay, Valerie," I finally respond. "I won't say anything to Ricky. But, real talk, if you're gonna keep playing him, I'm gonna need you to not tell me."

"Fair enough," Valerie says with a shrug. "Now let's go to practice. We've got a game Friday."

When Valerie and I walk into the Hi-Steppers rehearsal, everyone is already lined up, and Mrs. Vaughn, our coach, is in front blowing her whistle.

"Let me see a hamstring stretch from everyone!" Mrs. Vaughn shouts. Then she looks at me and Valerie. "And let's all give a round of applause to diva number one and diva number two, who finally decided to grace us with their presence!"

All of the Hi-Steppers, including Hope, stop stretching and start clapping. They're laughing too, although I don't see anything funny.

Mrs. Vaughn continues. "All right, divas, give me three

laps around the gym. Maybe next practice, you'll make it on time."

Valerie rolls her eyes at Mrs. Vaughn and we both start running. I take wide strides so that I can get away from Valerie. I need some time to think, plus since it's raining outside, the football team is warming up on the other side of the gym.

As I sprint past Romeo and crew, I think I hear a few snickers. Are they snickering at me? Do I have food in my teeth or something?

I'm nervous for my entire next lap until I get near the football players again. This time, Romeo winks at me and licks his lips. I give him a little wave, and because I'm not paying attention, I almost crash straight into the volley-ball net.

Valerie sprints past me and cracks up. "He's got you open, Ma."

"Nah." I try to sound like I don't care, but I'm pretty sure it's obvious that I do.

Valerie and I finish our final lap and run over to line up with the other Hi-Steppers. They've already started prac-ticing our step to an old cut by Notorious B.I.G. The step looks good, but I'm not sure that the band is going to be able to pull off the tune from "Hypnotize." They can barely play the school song and they play that at every game.

Just as we finish our last turn-stomp-kick combination, something breaks out on the other side of the gym.

Jewel and Kelani blurt out in unison, "FIGHT!!"

Everyone runs over to the crowd forming in the corner. Everyone except me. I've never been one for running up on fights. I'm definitely not trying to get hit by any stray punches, kicks, or bites. Yes, bites. Boys fight as dirty as girls sometimes.

I scan the crowd for Ricky, but I don't see him. We usually like to hang back and talk about how stupid everyone looks when they're chasing a fight. I know he's here, because I saw him when I was running my laps.

Then it hits me. . . . Could that be Ricky at the bottom of the pile?

Next thing I know, I'm squeezing through the crowd and tuning out Mrs. Vaughn's and Coach Rogers's yelling. The fight is finally breaking up with a group of boys holding Romeo's arms.

"Let me go! He deserves this beat down!"

Quickly, my eyes dart from Romeo to where he's glaring. Ricky is doubled over on the gymnasium floor, clutching his stomach.

I want to run to him, but something has my feet glued to the floor. Maybe it's the fear that if I help Ricky, then Romeo won't want another date with me. I feel like such a loser as I let the other football players help my best friend to his feet.

"Why y'all helping him up?" Romeo asks. "Especially you, Lance! You know he wants your QB spot. He ain't your boy."

Lance replies, "Of course he does. He should want it. He ain't getting it until I graduate, but he should still want it."

Coach Rogers snatches Romeo up by the collar, and says, "You need to cool off, son. In my office. Now!"

Since the fight is over, the crowd starts to disperse. The football team has to do one hundred extra drills since they got so rowdy. And Mrs. Vaughn steps out of the gym like she needs to cool off too.

Once Romeo is safely closed away in Coach Rogers's office, I sit down on the bench next to Ricky. He's bent over, with his head between his knees. I'm hating how pitiful he's looking right now, so I put one arm around his shoulders.

"You okay, Ricky?" I ask quietly.

His head snaps up as if he didn't know I was there. "Yeah, Gia. I'm cool."

For a moment we don't say anything. The tension is crazy. I mean, how do we even start this conversation? My best friend and my almost boyfriend were just fighting. Wow on top of wow.

"So . . . why were you and Romeo brawling?" I ask tentatively. "Did he foul you or something?"

Ricky lets out a soft, painful-sounding chuckle. "Girl, this is not basketball."

I'm so glad he laughs. I let out a laugh too. "Okay, I don't know the rules to the game. Sue me! I'm a nerd!"

"No you're not, Gia," Ricky says in an all-of-a-sudden serious tone. "There's nothing wrong with you."

"Ricky . . . what's up?"

He sits straight up and looks at me. "You don't really like Romeo, do you?"

"Well, I think so. I don't really know yet. Why?"

I really don't want to know the answer to this question, because now I'm getting the sneaky suspicion that Ricky's and Romeo's fight had something to do with me. That would make all of this worse.

Ricky shakes his head. "Because I think he doesn't really like you."

"What makes you think that?"

"It's just a feeling . . . I mean, him and his boys . . . well, I don't know, Gia. It's just a feeling, that's all. Why can't you just like Kevin? He likes you for real."

Now I just want to go straight upside Ricky's head and add to his injuries. "Are you trying to hurt my feelings or are you doing it by accident?"

Ricky bites his tongue and sighs. "Gia, Romeo dates girls like Valerie."

"And Valerie dates guys like Romeo, right?"

I get up and walk away from Ricky. He needs to let that go ahead and sink in. Yeah, I might not be Romeo's type, I know that. But while Ricky's got a feeling I'm getting played, I've got facts that *he's* getting played.

And guess what? I'm keeping the facts to myself.

★ 13 ★

"Is it good, honey?"

I nod my head twice while chewing the tuna casserole really, really slowly. Truth is Gwen can only cook two things. Spaghetti and chicken. Every time she tries to step outside the box, it's utter catastrophe.

"Well, I'm glad you like it. I've got to start practicing my cooking in case someone asks for my hand in marriage," she says with a smile.

Still chewing, I roll my eyes. "Like who, Mom?"

"You know who!" she exclaims, like I'm asking the world's dumbest question. "Elder LeRon."

What did I tell y'all? My mother gets real silly when it comes to men—even the ones who aren't feeling her. I hurry another bite of food in my mouth before I say something to get me slapped.

Gwen continues, "We've got our fourth date on Saturday."

"I thought you were going to the youth rally at church." Okay, since I'm planning on a little sneak action, I need to know exactly where Sister Gwen plans on spending her evening.

"Why are you so concerned about the youth rally?" Gwen asks. "You're going to your little sleepover, right?"

Hmm . . . gotta think fast. "I . . . uh . . . it's just that Pastor gets mad when our family doesn't represent."

"Mmm-hmm. If I didn't know any better, I'd think you were up to some mess."

Does she have a mess radar? I mean, seriously, either she's got some kind of lie detector attached to her brain, or the Lord is sending her direct signals, because she stays on my trail.

"Mom, please! Why do I always have to be up to something?"

Gwen slowly cracks a smile. "All right, Gia. I know I'm blessed to have a good child. I guess I'm just waiting for something crazy to happen."

"It's not gonna happen, Mom."

I feel super guilty about this conversation. Why can't Gwen be like normal mothers and just let me go out on a date? Why do I have to do all this lying and carrying on? This is so not me.

Gwen changes the subject. "So where's Tweety been all of a sudden? I haven't seen him lately?"

I smile because she remembers Tweety's gender. "Well, I just decided to give my boy Tweety a rest. I went through those clothes that Hope gave me, and there were actually a couple of cute outfits in there."

"And what about Ricky?" she asks. "Did you give him a rest too?"

Now why did she even have to go there? I know Gwen is talking about what went down in the youth Bible study class this evening. Ricky and I had gone out of our way not to speak to one another. And when Pastor told us to pick partners for an exercise, I didn't even complain when I ended up with extra-moisturized Kevin.

"Me and Ricky are cool," I try to explain. "He's just got football, and I've got the Hi-Steppers squad. We're busy."

I keep telling myself that I'm cool, that me and Ricky are cool, that it's *all* cool. But, real talk, after Ricky got into that fight two days ago, something is broken between us. I keep picking up my phone looking for a text saying, "I'm sorry."

But I haven't gotten it yet, and this is beyond crazy. Me and Ricky never stay on silent treatment this long. If Ricky would just tell me why he and Romeo were fighting, maybe we could squash this. But he hasn't and Romeo just blew me off when I asked him.

My cell phone buzzes on the table.

I pick it up quickly, hoping to see Ricky's number on the caller ID, but it's Romeo.

"Who is that calling so late?" Gwen asks.

"Valerie. She's probably calling about the sleepover. Can I take this in my bedroom?"

Gwen narrows her eyes. "Mmm-hmm."

I press the talk button on my phone and say, "Talk to me."

Gwen sits at the table with her arms folded, watching me with her hawk eyes as I walk out of the kitchen. I smile at her as I close my bedroom door.

"No, I *can't* wait for the sleepover!" I exclaim dramatically.

Romeo laughs on the other end of the phone. "You betta stop lying to your moms!"

"You don't worry about that," I reply with a giggle. "She needs to stay out of my bidness!"

"Gia, you are funny as what. So are we still on for Saturday?"

"Hmm . . . Don't you need to be thinking about winning that football game tomorrow?" I ask.

"Shorty, that's already in the bag. We're playing them lame fools over at West High this week."

"Oh, for real?"

The West High Sharks haven't won a game yet this season. I feel sorry for their cheerleaders. I wonder if they ever want to get up and cheer for the other team.

"Yep. Your BFF may even get some play action this week," Romeo says with a sarcastic chuckle.

"Who, Ricky?"

"Yeah. I don't think Coach Rogers is going to risk Lance getting hurt going into the play-offs. So he's probably gonna start Ricky."

I wonder if Ricky knows about this. Because if he knows he's starting at the game this week and he didn't call and tell me, then he must really not be talking to me. I might need to be calling him my ex-BFF.

I ask bluntly, "So are you and Ricky cool or what? What were y'all fighting about anyway?"

Romeo pauses for a long time before he answers my question. "We're cool. He tried to confront me on some gossip that he'd heard. I don't play that. Gossiping is for chicks."

"Okay . . ." All I'm thinking is *what gossip*? Was it about me?

"I just told your mans that if he had beef with me, then he needed to come see me. Period."

"Oh."

Gwen is knocking on my bedroom door. "Gia, get off that phone. It's a school night."

"Okay, Mom."

Romeo asks, "You gotta go, shorty?"

"Yeah. I'll see you tomorrow."

"All right then."

I hang up the phone and consider calling Ricky real quick, but I'm trying not to irk Gwen at all between now and Saturday. I don't want to give her a reason to revoke permission for the sleepover . . . er . . . date.

So, instead of calling I send Ricky a text message:

Yo. Heard u r starting on Friday! Congrats. Lata.

★14★

I've been dreading this day since the school year started, and it's finally here. I know what you're thinking. What day, right? Well, sit tight 'cause I'm about to fill you in on my pain.

Halfway into the quarter our phys ed class changes from indoor field hockey, volleyball, and three-on-three basketball to swimming. We trade the funky smell of the girls gym locker for chlorine, and we'll swim laps and learn to dive from the diving board.

Seems like no big deal, right? Umm . . . wrong.

It's not the actual swimming that gets to me, because I'm a great swimmer. I already know all the strokes Ms. Dixon is going to teach, so it's going to be an easy A. And it's not my hair, because my synthetic ponytail clips on and off with the quickness.

So what is the problem?

Imagine all ninety pounds of me in a swimsuit. An all

black one-piece swimsuit provided by the school. I'm talk-ing about my super skinny legs and my absence of booty and boobs all in one vision. Yeah, take that mental pic-ture and feel my pain.

To make it even worse, our swimming class is coed. That is so unnecessary. I mean, what are they thinking? I may try to make a case to the principal based on rising teen pregnancy rates.

But until that happens, I have to do the walk of shame to the ice-cold swimming pool. You would think they'd at least have a heated pool, but that would be another no.

I'm sitting on the locker room bench, in full foolish swim attire, waiting to be humiliated beyond reason. Hope is in my class too, and she along with Jewel and Kelani are looking at their reflections in the mirror.

Hope pulls her hair into a high ponytail and asks, "Do you think we'll have to go under the water today? I don't want to get my hair wet."

"I'm not getting my hair wet for the entire semester, why you playing!" Kelani replies.

I can't resist asking a question. "So you would just fail the class, because you don't want to mess up your hair?"

All three of them look at me like I've just asked the dumbest question in the world. I shrug and stuff my back-pack into the open locker in front of me.

"Anyway," Jewel says, dismissing my question, "I wish they would let us wear our own swimsuits. I've got a cute two-piece, with boy-short bottoms, that puts my booty on swole."

Wow on top of wow. Maybe I should be happy they're making us wear these grandma swimming suits. I'd look even worse with a two-piece. Because, yeah, my booty would be the opposite of swole.

The warning bell rings, so everyone heads for the pool. Surprisingly, I'm not the only girl stressing over her body. A few girls with figures I'd kill for are trying to cover up because they think they look fat. The only ones not pressed at all are Hope, Kelani, and Jewel.

The aroma of chlorine fills my nostrils as we walk into the pool area. All of the boys are at the deep end, because their locker room is on the opposite side of the pool. I scan the crowd of them, hoping that Ricky is in the class.

Yay! I see him standing off to the side with his arms crossed. And aw dang, Romeo is in here too. I was hoping that the Lord would smile on me and spare me the embarrassment of having *him* see me in a swimsuit. Instead the Lord is not smiling, but smiting me like my name is Miriam or somebody.

You don't know who Miriam is? Okay, she's like Moses's sister and the Lord gave her leprosy or something for pretty much being a hater. Go to Sunday school!

As all the girls finally appear from the locker room, the boys, being their typical, ignorant selves, start whistling and yelling. How rude is that?

Ms. Dixon motions for everyone to join her on the bleachers, and the boys run toward her acting like the fools that they are. Someone falls headfirst into the pool and of course they all laugh some more.

While Ms. Dixon attends to the accident, I sit down on the bleachers behind Ricky. I sigh and then clear my throat, trying to get his attention. I know he hears me, but he's not turning around.

I blurt, "Ricky, did you get my text?"

He turns around slowly, like he's trying to think of an excuse. "Umm, yeah. Thanks."

Three words? That's it! I move next to him and ask, "Are you still mad about what I said about Valerie?"

Yeah, I had to break the ice. You can think I'm a chump if you want, but Ricky is my boy. He's the only one who I know is really down for me. Since I don't have a lot of friends in my repertoire, I need to keep the ones that actually like me. Ya feel me?

"No. I'm not mad," Ricky says. "I know you were just trying to turn that whole conversation around on me."

Now I'm confused. "What do you mean?" I ask.

"There's no reason why Valerie wouldn't date me. You just said that because of what I said about you and Romeo."

"And there's no reason why Romeo wouldn't date me!" I say furiously.

I must be a tad bit loud because one of Romeo's friends says, "How about the fact that you look like a chocolate Blow Pop?"

Another footballer named James adds, "Yeah! She's got that big ol' brown circle head and a stick for a body."

I narrow my eyes angrily and wait for Ricky to jump in and stick up for me. He is irritatingly silent, so I speak up for myself.

"Shut up, James!" I yell. "I'd rather look like a Blow Pop than Shrek and Donkey!"

Everybody cracks up at this, because James does look like a giant ogre. He's on the defensive line of the Long-fellow Spartans. His size is good on the football field but nowhere else.

"Hey, fall back my dude," Romeo says in my defense.

At Romeo's command, James and company immediately fall back. I'm glad Romeo went ahead and got my back, though, because he was going to have some serious explaining to do. Like Mr. Ricky Ricardo. He is most definitely not off the hook.

"Okay, settle down!" Ms. Dixon says. "I'm going to break you guys up into two groups. Swimmers and non-swimmers. If you know how to hold your breath under water and swim one lap in the pool, you're in the swimmers group."

There are moans mostly from the girls, because unless they're rocking some kind of braids, they are not going to be looking cute.

Ms. Dixon continues, "Everyone line up by the shallow end, so that I can see your skill level."

"But, Ms. Dixon! I have a game tonight and Hi-Steppers have to have their hair done," Kelani says.

"Do you think I care about your little hairstyle?" Ms. Dixon asks with much attitude.

I don't even know why Kelani would try to pull that with Ms. Dixon. Seriously, the woman wears her hair in a stingy little ponytail on the regular. The words *fabulous, glamorous,* or *style* are not in her vocab.

As we line up at the edge of the pool, I make sure I'm directly behind Ricky so that I can continue our conversation.

"So, you were just gonna let them clown me, Ricky?" I ask, directly in his ear.

He sighs like he's irritated or something. "Listen, Gia, if you want to keep this thing up with Romeo, that's on you."

"What do you mean, that's on me?"

"I mean when he has you looking foolish out here, do not come running to me," he says like he's stressed or irritated. " 'Cause I'm done with it."

Ooh! No he didn't. I am sooooooo close to bursting his bubble about how Mz. Valerie is playing him. If I'm going to be looking foolish, so is he.

Instead I say, "All right then, Ricky. It's cool."

It's Kelani's turn to do her lap. She steps gingerly into the water and stands there with her arms crossed. Ms. Dixon blows her whistle.

"Today, Kelani," she says, and blows her whistle a second time.

Kelani lies, "I don't know how to swim, plus this water is freezing. I think I have hypoglycemia."

"You mean hypothermia. And the water is fine. Get to swimming!" Ms. Dixon then blows her whistle, like Kelani is going to take off.

"But, Ms. Dixon! I don't know how to swim! I might drown."

"Yes you do," Ms. Dixon says. "I had you for ninth grade. Now, either you give me a lap or you can take yourself down to the principal's office."

Kelani rolls her eyes and starts to doggie paddle across the pool. She looks hilarious trying to keep her hair from getting splashed, but she's doing a good job of it.

At the end of her lap, she touches the top of her head and smiles. She's only wet the hair at the nape of her neck. She should be cool when she takes her ponytail down.

"Am I done?" Kelani asks Ms. Dixon.

"Yes, Kelani. You may exit the pool. Who's next?"

Before Kelani can move out of the way, Kevin runs and does a flying leap into the pool to start his lap. His splash drenches Kelani from head to toe. Kelani then bursts into tears, and everyone else bursts into laughter.

Everyone except me and Ricky. He looks back at me and we lock eyes—our faces saying more than our words ever will. I hope we'll get past this Valerie and Romeo thing, because I miss my best friend.

When did my life get so complicated?

★15★

"Well, don't you look cute!" Gwen exclaims as I stand in the center of the living room with my entire Hi-Steppers outfit on, white boots, lip gloss, and all.

She's never seen me fully suited up, because she's never been to one of the games. They fall the same night as her singles ministry meetings, and for the most part she's not about to miss one of those. She's says it's because her husband might be up in the spot.

But tonight, Gwen and her "future husband" are coming to the football game, because Pastor Stokes cancelled their meeting. Elder LeRon is sitting at our kitchen table eating the take-out chicken Gwen brought home.

"Isn't she adorable, Elder LeRon?" she asks.

He nods. "Yep. She looks just like you, Gwen."

Mom beams a smile over in his direction like he just

proposed or something. She is so gone off this dude, it's ri-darn-diculous. She's tripping.

Gwen asks, "So is Ricky coming over to walk you to the game?"

Why is she pressing the whole Ricky issue? Clearly, she must know that there is some drama going on, even if I'm not sharing the details. Why does she have to keep stressing me?

"Ricky is starting tonight," I say. "He's probably already at the school."

"Oh, well, you can ride over with me and Elder LeRon if you want."

I shake my head. I've already had more of Elder LeRon than I can bear. "I'm cool. I'll walk."

"All right, honey."

"As a matter of fact, I'm going to leave now, so I don't have to rush." Before Gwen can offer any other objections, I grab my gym bag and walk out the front door.

I don't know how I feel about Gwen bringing Elder LeRon to my game. It's not like he's my daddy or anything. I wanted her to come to see me alone, not with a date or future husband. She'll probably be in the stands spending the whole time flirting with him rather than watching me.

When I walk into the girls locker room, everyone has already arrived, even Hope, who's made up with Kelani, Jewel, and Valerie. Funny she hasn't tried to make up with me, though. I guess she's still salty because I'm on the A squad. Whatev.

"Ooo-OOO!" Valerie calls.

"Ooo-OOO!" is my response.

Valerie asks, "So are you ready for tomorrow night?"

Good question, but I don't know the answer. Am I ready to lie to my mom and sneak out on a date with the boy who hates my almost-ex-best friend? I don't know. How does one get ready for that?

"What's happening tomorrow night?" asks Hope's nosy behind.

"Oh, you can't speak, but you can be all up in my business?" I ask.

She rolls her eyes and answers, "Well, you didn't speak either."

"Maybe I didn't speak because you're constantly mean-mugging somebody," I answer truthfully.

Valerie steps between us. "Okay, girls, I'm gonna need y'all to put all that cousin rivalry to the side and act like Hi-Steppers. You all don't see me beefing with the other ladies."

Well, that's because the other girls happen to fear Valerie's wrath. Who's gonna beef with her when she can kick you off the A squad with the quickness? Most definitely not Jewel and Kelani.

Hope says, "She's right, Gia. I'm sorry for mean-mugging you."

She totally catches me off guard with this. I can't even think of anything sarcastic to say. And that is uncommon, 'cause a girl like me always has a quip. No . . . I am not defining that word. *Hooked on Phonics,* boo. Buy it, use it, embrace it.

"Yeah, I'm sorry too," I say, although I don't really feel

like I have something to be sorry about. I just want all the hate to stop, and plus I've got more important things to worry about than Hope's issues.

Valerie puts her arms around both of us. "See how easy that was? Hi-Stepper love!"

"So are you going to tell me your plans for the weekend now?" Hope asks.

Oh, so that's what the apology was all about. Boo!

"Um . . . no," I answer.

Valerie laughs. "Well, Hope, you *did* play her the last time, so I don't know why you expect her to be telling you her business."

The entire Hi-Stepper squad bursts into laughter, including me. Truth is truth. It's going to take a long time for me to trust Hope again. It may never happen.

Most of the girls leave the locker room and head for the bleachers. They want plenty of time to flirt with the football players and look cute before the game starts. I still have to put some extra shine on my boots, though, so I sit down on the bench.

Hope stays behind too and surprises me by sitting down next to me. She says, "Gia, I asked you about your weekend because I heard something foul."

"About me?"

She nods. "Yeah. I heard Romeo has been talking real reckless."

This gets my attention. I wonder if it has anything to do with his and Ricky's fight.

I ask, "Reckless how?"

"I heard he said that he's only talking to you because Valerie told him you wanted to give it up."

Wait a minute. What? Give *what* up? I feel my anger rising.

Since I'm sitting here with my mouth hanging open, Hope continues, "He says that he's gonna tap that on Saturday night."

Finally, my mouth forms words. "Did you actually hear him say this?"

"No, but Jewel and Kelani said . . ."

I roll my eyes. That's all I needed to hear. I suck my teeth and answer, "For real, Hope? I can't believe you're coming to me with something from those dummies."

"But I don't think they were lying!" she exclaims.

I slick some Vaseline on the toe of my boot and stand up. "And for your information, I'm spending the night at Valerie's on Saturday."

Hope raises her eyebrow like she doesn't believe me. "Gia, you're changing. And it's not for the better. You need to check yourself, boo."

"I never knew you were such a hater," I answer, and stomp out of the locker room.

Oh no, she didn't try to go there about somebody changing! How about how she changed once she got some new clothes and a hairstyle? What about how she stopped being my friend once we got to high school?

Maybe it's time for me to change. Everyone else around me is changing. Ricky is chasing girls, getting into fights and letting people call him Rick. He's totally different. Well, I'm about to give them a new and improved Gia Stokes. And the new and improved me has a boyfriend. Deal with it!

Valerie stops me on my way out to the football field. "What were you and Hope talking about?"

"Nothing. Absolutely nothing."

I push past Valerie as well, and go up into the bleachers with the marching band. I plop down next to a random flute player and search the stands.

There's Gwen and Elder LeRon. They've got their cups of hot cocoa and boxes of popcorn. They're looking real datelike and not like a mother coming to cheer her daughter on. I shake my head in disgust.

I look down at the field to see if any of the football players have come out. Usually, a few of them trickle into the stands to say hello to their people and flirt with the girls before the game starts.

I see Romeo, and he's waving at me. I wave back, but after my conversation with Hope I'm not excited at all about him showing me some attention. He's making his way up the steps to where I'm sitting.

"Hey, lil' shorty. What's poppin'?" Romeo asks with an incredibly cute smile. His lips are so unbelievably unchapped. It makes absolutely no sense.

Even though I'm suspicious of him now with all of Ricky's and Hope's warnings, I still crack a smile too. "Hey, Romeo."

He grabs my hand and I feel my stomach lurch. He's taking my hand right out here in the open where everyone can see?

"Come on," he says. "I want you to meet my moms."

He wants me to meet his mother! Oh my goodness. Okay, the haterific duo of Ricky and Hope can just fall back. If he wants me to meet his mother, then he must really like me. I don't care what they say.

But I do care about Gwen casting some serious side-eye action over in my direction. Hmm . . . I'm gonna have to deal with her in a minute. Maybe this is not such a good idea.

"Hey, baby! Over here!" a young woman sitting in the bleachers shouts. It looks like she's waving at Romeo.

"Is that your sister?" I ask.

Romeo laughs. "Naw, that's Moms."

I feel my stomach do a huge flip-flop. Romeo's mother looks about twenty-three years old. I know that she has to be older than that, but you can't tell by looking at her. She's wearing a two-story, quick-weave ponytail. And I kid you not, there is a champagne glass glued in the middle of it. She has on a short, gold Baby Phat jacket with a furry hood and Apple Bottoms jeans.

Romeo puts his hand on my back and pushes me toward his mother. Then he says, "Ma, this is Gia. She's a Hi-Stepper."

"Okay, okay. I see you. I see you!" Romeo's mother responds.

I wonder if she has some kind of strange illness that makes her repeat everything she says. She shoves her full set of acrylic nails in my face, so I guess that means I'm supposed to shake her hand.

"I'm Diane," she says. "You kickin' it with my son?"

I nod. "Yes, ma'am."

"Ooh, girl, don't you be 'yes ma'am-ing' me! I am not a ma'am."

"Okay . . ."

Diane leans in really close and says quietly, "You make sure you tell my son to use some protection. I don't want any grandbabies."

My eyes get so wide that I'm sure they're about ready to fall out of my head. Romeo laughs, but I'm not finding anything funny. Me no likee this woman. First of all, do I even *look* like I'm giving it up? No, ma'am.

Since this conversation is never going to make it to a good place, I say, "It was nice meeting you, Ms. Diane. I've got to go and line up with the other Hi-Steppers."

"All right then, girl. You workin' them boots with your little skinny legs. Work it! Work it!" Ms. Diane punctuates all this by putting both hands in the air. Waving them like she just don't care. Umm . . . yeah.

Romeo, still laughing, kisses his mom on the cheek. Then he does the unthinkable and throws his arm around my shoulder as we walk away. He does this in clear view of Gwen. I can just feel her eyes burning a hole through my ponytail and right into my skull.

When I think I'm about to escape with no consequences, I hear a voice from the bleachers. "GIA!!!"

"See what you did!" I hiss at Romeo. "Now, come on. You've got to meet Gwen."

"Fo' sho'! Don't worry, lil' mama. I got this." This dude's swagger is unreasonable. I just hope he knows what he's doing. Kung Fu Gwen might be ready to knock somebody out.

We trudge up the bleacher steps to where Gwen and Elder LeRon are sitting. A brief glance at Gwen tells me that she is not happy. Her arms are crossed and she's frowning deeply. *Lord, please don't let her embarrass me.*

"Gia, who is this?" Gwen asks when Romeo and I stop in front of her.

Romeo extends his hand politely. "I'm Gia's friend Romeo, ma'am."

"Romeo? Did your mama name you that or is that what these little girls around here call you?"

I gasp in horror. No she didn't just clown his name. Why is the Lord not hearing my cries?

"Yes, ma'am, it's my given name," Romeo replies with a chuckle. At least he's being a good sport about it.

"Mom, Romeo is on the football team."

Gwen looks him up and down. "Well, that's obvious since he's wearing the uniform."

"What church do you go to?" Elder LeRon asks.

Okay, did he seriously just question someone like he's my daddy? He better fall back and recognize his spot—boyfriend. That's it. I'm taking deep breaths now to keep from exploding.

Romeo replies, "I attend New Hope Missionary Baptist Church, where Reverend James Wilkinson is my pastor."

Uh-oh! Go 'head, Romeo. I underestimated him on his impress-the-parents skills. Elder LeRon seems satisfied, but Gwen is still not pleased.

Gwen asks, "So you're introducing my daughter to your mother? Are you dating?"

"We're only friends right now, Mrs. Stokes," Romeo says with a reassuring smile. "I think we're too young to date, don't you?"

Gwen rolls her eyes and throws one hand up. "Boy, don't try to play me."

"Ma'am?" Romeo asks.

Oh no. He's laying it on too thick. Bring it back, Romeo! Bring it back! Gwen has a mess radar. I've got to rescue him.

I say, "Mom, the game is about to start. We've got to go."

"Mmm-hmm. You get your little behind home immediately following the game. We need to have a talk."

"Okay, Mom."

As Romeo and I head for the field, he asks, "Did I do okay?"

"If you see me tomorrow night, you'll know," I say. "She just might lock me away forever after that."

Romeo smiles and takes my hand. "For real, shorty? 'Cause I have big plans for us."

I swallow hard. Big plans? I'm not comfortable with his plans or his holding my hand all out in public. Aside from the fact that Gwen has her X-ray vision trained on me, we've only been on one date and that wasn't even a real date. Are you supposed to have public displays of affection after one date? Me thinks no.

Romeo runs onto the field with the rest of the team and leaves me standing with the marching band. I steal a look up in Gwen's direction and girlfriend is staring me down. Hard.

I'm thinking my social life is probably over. So much for popularity.

★16★

I take my time walking home from the game, because I don't want to face Gwen. I could feel her giving me the evil side eye for the entire game. Even when the Hi-Steppers were out on the field performing, I could feel Gwen glaring at me.

I already know what it's gonna be. She'll want to know all about Romeo and she'll probably ground me on general principle.

I don't know why I got so caught up when Romeo wanted to introduce me to his mother. I didn't even think about the Gwen factor. Maybe I need for this thing between me and Romeo to be real and not something everyone thinks I'm making up in my imagination.

One good thing that happened tonight was that Ricky threw four touchdown passes. It was awesome how the crowd went crazy. Even Lance Rogers was giving Ricky props.

I wanted to congratulate Ricky on having a great game, but Valerie was all over him. I guess her other dude isn't a football player.

As I walk down our street, my steps get slower and slower until I'm barely moving at all. The street is quiet except for some silly dog who's howling at the sky. The moon isn't even all the way out yet and that dumb dog is howling.

It's gonna be me howling if I don't say exactly what Gwen wants to hear.

In my mind, I try to plan my answers to her questions. In no way can I make Romeo seem like he's my boo or anything important. He has to have complete Ricky status. If I say the wrong thing, I can forget about leaving the house tomorrow night.

As quietly as possible, I walk up the creaky steps to our duplex. When I get to the last step, my boot gets caught on a broken piece of wood and I fly across the porch and into the door. Raggedy house!

All the lights go on in the living room, so I can forget about Gwen being asleep. I was hoping that her little boyfriend's car would still be in the driveway. She wouldn't dare show her claws in front of Elder LeRon. At least I don't think she would, but I was alarmed at the game, because I thought she was about to body slam Romeo.

I open the front door and Gwen is standing front and center in her robe with both hands on her hips. She's looking right crazy, with a scary looking frown and beads of sweat on her forehead.

"What took you so long?" she asks angrily. "Didn't I tell you to come straight home after the game?"

"I did. I was just walking slowly, I guess."

She looks me up and down and then points to the couch. "Have a seat, Miss Thang."

Whenever she calls me Miss Thang it's because she thinks I'm doing dirt. I'm afraid that no matter what I say, she isn't going to believe me. I sit down on the couch and look at my feet. I can't look at her face because she's giving me the evil eye.

"So who is Romeo?" she asks point-blank.

"He's just a friend, Mom."

"Then why have I never heard about him? Surely, you and Ricky would've had him around before now. He would've visited us at church or something. I think you're running game."

I clear my throat, trying to stall so my brain can come up with an answer that makes sense and doesn't sound like a lie. "We just started hanging out this year. He's in my French class."

"Is he the reason for all this?" Gwen asks as she flips my ponytail to the side.

I reply, "No, Mom. Valerie wanted me to look like a Hi-Stepper, that's all."

Gwen sighs and sits down next to me. She looks sad and tired, like she's been dreading this moment my entire life. I brace myself for the inevitable mother-daughter talk.

Calmly, she says, "Gia, it scared me when I saw that boy introducing you to his mother."

"But why?"

"Because this is all going too quickly. Boys aren't supposed to be chasing you down yet."

I object. "Mom, boys *aren't* chasing me down. I'm mostly invisible."

She shakes her head and responds. "I know what I saw in that Romeo's eyes. He's just like most of the boys out here, Gia."

"He's only after one thing, right?" I finish her thought for her. Maybe that will help to speed up this conversation.

Gwen sucks her teeth. "You think you're so smart, don't you? Straight A's won't help you when some boy has you hemmed up and is kissing on you and making you feel things you've never felt before."

I squirm uncomfortably in my seat, remembering how Romeo made me feel when he took my hand at the football game. She's right. I'd never felt anything like that before.

Gwen continues, "You'll think that you have your head on straight; then next thing you know, you will have given up your virginity to some boy who doesn't even care about you."

"Is that what happened to you, Mom?" I ask quietly.

Tears form in my mother's eyes. "Yes, Gia. That's exactly what happened to me. And as much as I love you, I would never want you to be a teenage mom. Or worse, get a disease that never goes away."

"Mom. I'm not having sex, and I don't plan on it. I don't even have a boyfriend, so you don't have to worry."

She sighs. "Gia, no matter what words come out of your mouth, I'm still going to worry. I don't want you to be stupid."

"Okay, Mom. I hear you."

"I want you to listen," she says. Then she touches her

finger to my chest. "And I want it to get in here. In your heart."

I nod slowly, trying not to burst into tears from guilt. "Okay."

"And don't ever forget that you belong to Christ, Gia. Do you know how special that is? Don't just give yourself away to someone who doesn't deserve it. You're a daughter of the King."

"Yes, ma'am."

Gwen crosses her fingers and puts them in her lap. "So . . . Ricky had four touchdowns, huh?"

I let out a sigh of relief. The lecture must be over. "Yes, Ricky was really good."

"Doesn't he usually walk you home?" she asks.

"Yes, but he went to IHOP with everyone. I had to come straight home, remember?"

She smiles. "Right. Well, you better get to bed. You've got to be at Mother Cranford's early in the morning."

"Okay. Is it all right if I just go over to Valerie's house after Mother Cranford's?"

Gwen looks confused for a moment, and then says, "Oh, that sleepover thing. I guess so."

Gwen stands and starts toward her bedroom. Before she walks through her door, she says, "Don't forget what I said, Gia."

"Okay, Mom."

I'm not going to forget what my mom just said, or what Ricky or Hope said either. But they are not in my shoes. There is nothing that anyone can say that will stop me from going out on this date with Romeo.

★17★

Do you know the definition of *high dusting*? No? Neither did I until I showed up at Mother Cranford's house today. As soon as I walked through the door, she handed me a bucket of rags and a can of furniture polish.

"What's this for?" I asked.

"Baby, I haven't been able to do any high dusting in months," Mother Cranford said. "I bet there's about a foot of dust on the tops of my bookcases and china cabinets. Won't you be a dear and wipe them down for me?"

So now, I'm perched on a stepladder with a scarf tied around my head, wiping a gang of dust off furniture. This is not how I intended to spend this Saturday afternoon. I was supposed to be fixing a little lunch, reading a Bible verse or two and chillaxin'. All this hard labor is for the birds. Plus, I know I'm gonna get dust up in this ponytail.

Mother Cranford sits in her recliner with a blanket on her lap. She says, "I see you got yourself a new hairdo."

That you're trying to destroy! "Yes, Mother Cranford. Do you like it?"

"Well, I think I liked the afro puffs better. They suited your pretty face."

"I was sick of that hairstyle. I've had it since kindergarten. I needed a change."

Mother Cranford pauses for a moment, and then says, "Sometimes we change stuff that don't need changin'."

Oh, for crying out loud! Not Mother Cranford too! Everybody is so full of advice these days. I'm sick to death of everyone always trying to tell me something. Did they all think my life was fine when I was a complete geek with only one friend to my name? Where was everyone's advice then? Exactly!

"Well, I like it this way, Mother."

"You don't have to get all that sass in your tone, baby. I'm just saying what I know."

Sass? I guess I did just get a little bit extra smart right then. "I'm sorry."

Mother Cranford grunts her reply and turns on the television with her remote control. She finds her favorite show, *Walker, Texas Ranger.* Why did I have to go and get sassy? Now, not only am I going to be covered in dust, but I'll have to listen to Chuck Norris's gems of wisdom for the entire time.

My cell phone buzzes on my hip, so I take a seat on the stepladder to read the text message. U comin 2 the youth rally?

The text is from Ricky. I quickly type a response: nope goin' 2 val's.

I typed that so easily that it scares me a little. It's never been this easy for me to lie to anyone, especially to my mom and my best friend. I want to tell Ricky about my date, but I don't trust him to keep it quiet, not since he and Romeo aren't cool anymore.

"I'm not paying you to sit around and punch buttons on that phone," Mother Cranford says with much attitude. Looks like Mother Crabapple has returned. She better not try to pinch me. I'm not playing.

"Yes, Mother Cranford."

I put my phone away and get back to the dust bunnies. Did she say she hadn't gotten any dusting done in months? Try years. I think I just wiped away some dirt from the Civil War.

After hours of backbreaking work and listening to the *Walker, Texas Ranger* marathon, I'm finally finished. Not a moment too soon, either, because it's almost time for Valerie to pick me up.

I say, "Mother Cranford, I've cleaned the tops of everything and polished the furniture too."

Mother Cranford replies, "Since I can't get up there and inspect it, I'm going to take your word for it."

I peek out the front curtains and see that Valerie has not yet arrived. "Is there anything else you want me to do? Do you want me to heat up one of your frozen dinners?"

She shakes her head slowly, still wearing her frown from earlier. "Some of the young folk from the church are bringing me a plate of barbeque from the youth rally."

"Oh, okay then," I reply as I look out the window again.

"Why do you keep looking out that window?"

"I'm just waiting on my ride. She should be here any minute."

"Well, set yourself down on the sofa and wait like you got some sense. The Bible says that the Lord hates feet that be swift in running to mischief! Hey, glory! Hallelujah."

I didn't mean for Mother Cranford to go over into the spirit realm, but she's sitting there fanning herself like she just got a touch of the Holy Spirit. But seriously, what makes her think I'm running to mischief? Is the Lord telling Mother Cranford my business too?

At last, I hear Valerie's horn. I jump up and grab my overnight bag. "That's my ride, Mother Cranford. I'm leaving, okay?"

"Don't you want to get paid?" she asks.

"Oh, yes, of course."

Mother Cranford narrows her eyes suspiciously. "Bring me my purse."

As I go to get her bag from the dining room table, Mother Cranford continues. "I don't know anybody who works that hard all day, and then doesn't ask about the pay. Your mind is somewhere else, gal."

Yes, she's absolutely right. My mind is outside of this dusty, old-rerun-watching dungeon and onto my first real date with Romeo. I'm trying to be up out of here, real talk.

I hand Mother Cranford her purse and she commences to digging through napkins, tissues, and receipts. I don't know how she finds anything up in that labyrinth (Hooked on Phonics, boo).

"You want a peppermint?" she asks as she hands me

an ancient-looking peppermint ball. Why do church mothers always have peppermints in their purses?

I take the piece of candy and say thank you. I try to unwrap it, but it's so old that it's sticking to the paper and there are little pieces of lint and hair on one side.

I put the piece of candy in my pocket and say, "I'll just save this for later."

Valerie toots again. I open the door and shout, "Just a second!"

"Close that door!" Mother Cranford fusses. "You letting all my heat out."

I shut the door and go back over to Mother Cranford's recliner. She hands me two crumpled up twenty-dollar bills.

"Thank you, Mother Cranford," I say breathlessly. I'm ready to go!

"You make sure you give the Lord His tithes. Because if you don't . . ."

Oh no! She's about to start preaching again! "I know, Mother Cranford! I know all about giving back to the Lord," I say quickly, hoping to turn her off before she gets started.

"All right then. I'll see you next Wednesday. Bring your little friend Ricardo too. That is a God-fearing young man right there."

I make a mad dash for the door, before Mother Cranford thinks of anything else to say or preach about. "Bye, Mother Cranford."

Valerie rolls her eyes as I get into the front seat of her car. "What took you so long?"

"Mother Cranford was tripping!"

"And why are you covered in dirt? I hope you're not wearing that on your date!" Valerie says as she wipes a streak of dust off my Tweety T-shirt.

"No. I'm not wearing this. I need to hurry and get to your house so I can shower."

Valerie nods and replies. "So, this is how we're going to do this. We're going to tell my Mom that we're going to the mall."

"Okay . . ."

"Then I'm going to drop you off and go with Brad to a party at his older sister's sorority house."

"How will I get back to your house?" I ask.

"Romeo will drop you off, silly. If I'm back before you, I'll wait in my car until you show up. But it better not be after midnight. I'm not getting in trouble for you."

I say, "I thought you called off your date with Brad so that you could help me."

"I *am* helping you! It turned out that I can help you and go out on my date too."

"I thought you'd be all about Ricky after the game yesterday," I say, the anger rising in my voice.

Valerie smiles. "Yes, Rick did come up in the rankings after that game. Looks like he might become the starting QB after all. Then, he can be my main dude."

"But not your only dude?" I ask.

"I'm too young to have only one boyfriend!" Valerie exclaims with a laugh. "But I'll claim him, though."

I sit back in my seat with my arms folded. Valerie sounds downright shady. I can't help but feel like I'm setting myself up to get played by dealing with her. Hope's warning is blaring in my mind.

"So, did you have anything to do with Romeo and I getting hooked up?" I ask.

She replies, "Who told you that?"

"I'm just asking. It seemed so sudden, that's all."

"Well, I wasn't going to tell you this," Valerie says, "but Romeo did ask me about you when he was about to holla at you."

"And what did you say?"

"I told him that you were a good Hi-Stepper and that you had much potential to be fly."

"That's all?"

"That's all."

I suck my teeth and twist my lips to the side. Valerie is leaving something out. I don't believe her.

I don't get the chance to interrogate Valerie further because we pull up to her house. Valerie's mother is on their porch, sweeping dirt into a little dustpan. She smiles up at us, looking like a carbon copy of her daughter.

"Hola, Val . . . and Val's little friend."

"Hello, ma'am. I'm Gia."

Valerie laughs. "Mami, you remember Gia. She had the little afros."

Valerie's mother scrunches her nose. "Sí, I remember that dreadful hairstyle. I'm so happy you let Valerie talk you into a makeover."

I feel some smart aleck reply on the tip of my tongue, so I don't open my mouth. I just smile like a sweet little robot clone of myself.

Valerie says, "Mami, Gia's going to change clothes and

then we're going to the mall. We won't be back until late, but I won't miss curfew."

"Okay, mija."

Why can't Gwen be like this? Why can't I just go where I want without having to answer any questions?

Upstairs in Valerie's room as she fixes my hair, I say, "Valerie, you are so lucky. Your mom is cool."

"Yeah, she is. But she don't play about curfew. You better be here by midnight, or I'm walking in the house and I will throw you under the bus with the quickness."

She turns me around to face the mirror. "There," she says. "You're looking cute again."

Valerie has slicked my ponytail up on one side and the baby hair is poppin'. She's added some glitter eye shadow and lip gloss too. Along with my snug V-neck sweater and skinny jeans, I'm looking real fresh.

All the way to the mall, Valerie talks on her cell phone to Brad. She's getting on my nerves with that, but I try not to think about it. Ricky thinks he's all that, so why should I care if he's getting played? Plus, I don't want to be in a bad mood when I meet Romeo.

Valerie drops me off in front of the movie theater, where Romeo is waiting. He smiles and licks his lips as soon as he sees me.

"Dang, shorty. You lookin' good!" he says.

He is always so full of compliments, isn't he? Does it matter that he also always looks like he's about to eat me alive?

"Thanks, Romeo," I say.

I wave to Valerie to let her know she can leave. Then I ask Romeo, "Are you going to drop me off back over Valerie's house?"

"Fo' sho'. But are you ready for the night to be over already?" Romeo asks.

A smile spreads across my face. "Of course not."

"You want something to eat?" Romeo asks.

"I could eat."

Romeo puts his arm around my waist and leads me into the mall. Immediately my body tenses under his touch.

"Relax, shorty," he says. "I don't bite."

"I'm cool," I reply. That's a lie, but I don't want him to think I'm lame.

Romeo points to a table in the middle of the food court. "Sit down right here. I'm gonna get some pizza and Pepsi. Is that all right with you?"

"Yeah, that's cool."

Romeo laughs. "Everything's cool, huh?"

I nod and laugh with him. I'm just so nervous. Scared that I'm gonna say or do something stupid to make him not want to be seen with me.

After a short time, Romeo comes back with a tray holding two slices of pizza and two cups. "I hope you like pepperoni," he says.

"I do. I love pepperoni," I reply.

Romeo takes a huge bite out of his pizza slice and then says, "So, I was thinking that maybe we won't go see the movie. Why don't we just take a drive to Mentor Headlands and look at the lake."

"Because it's not swimming weather," I object.

Romeo laughs at me. "It's not that cold yet! It's in the fifties tonight. It's really peaceful out there in the dark with the stars and moon shining."

I search Romeo's face for a sign that he's trying to play me. He seems sincere, I guess, but I'm not one hundred percent sure.

"I guess it'll be all right," I say reluctantly.

"You sound scared, shorty. Why?"

"Because I don't really know why you like me, Romeo. I've heard some things, and they've got me doubting all this."

Romeo replies, "Oh, now I see what's up. Ricardo's been blocking."

"It hasn't just been Ricky," I say matter-of-factly. "Why don't you just tell me why you like me, and it'll make me feel better."

"I like you 'cause you're smart and cute, and you ain't been with every dude in the school. Why do you like me, ma?"

I clear my throat, trying to stall. Why do I like him again? Um . . . er . . . uh . . . Why can't I think of any good reasons?

After a long pause, I reply, "Romeo, you're cool and popular and fresh-to-death."

"Are those the only reasons?" he asks.

"Do I need any more?"

Romeo laughs. "No. But you don't think I'm sexy? Do you need to see my six-pack?"

Sexy? Hmm . . . I'm not sure I know the definition of sexy. Actually, that word is not in my vocab. If Gwen heard him asking me this, she'd knock his head off. No. She'd probably knock my head off and then use my broken head to knock Romeo out.

I smile nervously. "Romeo, I'm not really on that. Do you know what I mean?"

He looks disappointed. Oh well. He finishes off his slice of pizza and wipes his hand on the napkin.

"So what's up?" he asks. "You wanna go to the lake or not?"

"I guess so. I just have to be back at Valerie's house by midnight."

Romeo's smile finally returns. "Not a problem. Let's get out of here."

We walk out of the mall and into the parking lot. Romeo was right. It is pretty warm out here for October. By the end of the month, though, it'll be wintertime. I can't remember the last time it was warm on Halloween.

Romeo puts his arm around my shoulders and says, "Come here, ma."

Romeo being all up on me like this is making me nervous. We're in Mentor, and that's about an hour away from home, not the other side of the world. What if I run into one of the church members or one of my mama's nosy friends? That would be right tragic.

Romeo unlocks the car doors of a fresh, black 2008 Chevy Impala. The chrome rims on the tires seem to shine brighter as we get closer to the car.

"Is this your ride?" I ask.

"I wish. This is my cousin's car. He let me use it tonight, especially for our date."

"Are you trying to impress me?" I ask.

"Fo' sho'."

I feel a flutter in my stomach as he opens the passenger side door for me to climb in. He's trying to impress me?

Wow! Romeo jumps in on his side and puts the car in reverse. Then he looks over at me and frowns.

"Are you gonna buckle up?" he asks.

"Oh, yeah! Of course."

And he's concerned about my safety. Wow again. He's getting ready to be my boo for real.

After ten minutes of driving, we pull into the park that leads to the beach, and it's deserted. Of course it's deserted, because nobody goes to the lake this time of year! For a quick second, the fact that there are no other cars anywhere around worries me.

Romeo puts the car into park and shuffles through a stack of CDs. He puts in Alicia Keys and plays my fave song, "Teenage Love Affair." Is he trying to tell me something? I'm thinking yeah.

The sky is overcast and full of big fluffy snow clouds. "So much for the moon and stars," I say as I look out the window.

"Who needs that, when I can look at you, shorty?"

I suck my teeth and reply, "Quit playing, Romeo. I know you don't think I'm 'bout to fall for that. Do I look lame to you?"

"I'm serious, Gia," he says with a grin. "I've been checking for you since ninth grade."

"Really?" I ask, not actually believing all this.

"Really."

"Well, what took you so long to say something?"

Romeo grabs the steering wheel with both hands, licks his lips and responds, "First of all, I thought you were Ricardo's girl. Second . . . I didn't think you'd like me because you're so smart."

"No lie?"

"I'm serious, shorty. I thought you'd take me for a dumb jock or something."

I lean back in my seat and try to take this all in. Romeo is sitting here telling me that he's been digging me since last year, Tweety, afro puffs, and all. All ninety pounds in baggy jeans and Payless shoes? Wow.

But just when I'm getting ready to object, Romeo leans over and kisses me on my mouth.

"I've been waiting to do that all night," he says.

Dang! Why didn't he warn me that he was going to do that? It happened so fast that I didn't get a chance to enjoy it. But still, I'm speechless.

Romeo asks, "Are you gonna say anything?"

I shake my head. Usually, I *do* have something to say about everything. This time, I have no words.

So he kisses me again. This time he swiftly slips his hand under my jacket where there would be a breast if I didn't have the body of a ten-year-old. Just as swiftly, I push him away.

"You gotta back that up, Romeo. I'm not on that," I say. And I mean it.

"Come on, baby girl. You know what it is."

I narrow my eyes angrily and reply, "Umm, no. I don't know what you *think* it is, but I didn't come here to let you freak me."

Romeo opens his car door and gets out. He sits down on the hood of the car like he's thinking about something. I hope he's using his brain to figure out how to get me to Valerie's house.

I get out of the car too. I stand in front of Romeo with my hands on my hips and ask, "Romeo, is this the only reason why you brought me out here?"

Romeo rolls his eyes and exhales. "Man, I should've known."

"You're right. You should've known that I wasn't havin' this. I think you need to take me back to Valerie's house."

"Dang, shorty! You trippin' for real. Valerie said you were down." Romeo says this and then gets the "oops" look on his face like he said something that he shouldn't have said.

"Valerie said what?"

"Man, nothing!" Romeo replies as he jumps back into the car.

I need to stay out here and catch my breath for a minute. I take a few steps toward the water, trying to calm down. First of all, why are Romeo and Valerie having conversations about me? And Valerie said I was down?

What's really going on?

Then, I hear the gravel under Romeo's tires start to crunch like he's pulling off. Wait a minute. He is pulling off.

"What are you doing?" I yell.

Romeo rolls down his window. "You played me, coming all the way out here like you didn't know what it was. Now, I'm about to play you. I'm out to my house."

Time seems to have stopped as I'm standing here looking foolish. Romeo peels out with his tires squealing. I cannot believe he's left me stranded at the lake, just 'cause I wouldn't let him touch all over me. I can't believe I thought he was the business.

I am straight kicking myself for not listening to Ricky and Hope. Even Gwen knew what was up. How could I be so stupid? Not only am I sitting here stranded, but now I'm gonna get in trouble too? I pull out my cell phone and try to call Valerie. Naturally, it goes straight to voice mail.

I cannot call Gwen. I just can't. If I do, my life as I know it will be over. No Hi-Steppers, no sleepovers, no job, no ponytail. I'd be grounded until the end of time.

So, as much as I hate to do this, I dial Ricky's number. After a few rings, he answers, "Hello."

I hear lots of noise in the background. "Hey, Ricky, it's me, Gia."

"Oh, hey. What's up?"

"Are you at church?" I ask.

"Yeah, I'm at the youth rally. You over Valerie's house?"

I inhale deeply and then exhale slowly. "Not exactly."

"Well, where are you? And what's wrong? You sound crazy."

"Ricky, can you do me a favor and move far away from wherever my mother might be?"

"Okay. Give me a sec."

I can tell that Ricky walks out of the auditorium because the noise dies. He says, "Okay, I'm good. What's up?"

"Ricky, I'm stranded out at Mentor Headlands. Do you think you can get someone to pick me up?"

"Someone like who?" he asks. "And why are you all the way in Mentor?"

"Umm . . . I came out here with Romeo."

All I hear is silence on the phone. I can't tell what Ricky is thinking because he's not saying anything at all.

"Ricky? You there?" I ask, thinking the call was dropped.

"Yeah, I'm here. So you and Romeo are all the way at Mentor Headlands, and you're stranded."

I do not like Ricky's tone. He sounds like he thinks he's my daddy or something. He needs to simmer all that action down. "I didn't say I was stranded with Romeo. He's . . . umm . . . he's not here."

Ricky says, "Did he leave you out there?"

"What were y'all doing way out by the beach? Gia, don't tell me you were out there letting him freak on you!"

I'm about to say something really ignorant to Ricky, when I hear Gwen in the background. "Are you talking to *my* Gia?" she asks. "Give me that phone!"

Ricky says, "Sorry, Gia . . ."

"Gia, where are you and what is Ricky talking about?" Gwen asks.

"I—I'm with Valerie, and we're stranded."

"Girl, you better quit lying to me now, before you make me cuss in the house of the Lord," she says. I can hear the anger in her voice and it chills me to the bone.

"I am stranded. I'm out at the beach, in Mentor," I say as I try to choke back a sob.

"What kind of car are you in?"

"I'm not in a car. I'm just standing here."

"What? Gia, you're talking real stupid right now," Gwen says, sounding mad on top of mad. "You're with that little fool I met at the football game, aren't you?"

"I was . . . but he left me out here," I say quietly.

I guess she hands the phone back to Ricky, because he says, "Umm . . . I think your mom and Elder LeRon are gonna go pick you up."

"Thanks a lot, Ricky."

"I'm sorry."

I press the "end" button on my phone. What a disaster! The tears that pour from my eyes feel like little hot rivers against my cold face.

Suddenly, the darkness makes me scared. The cloudy sky is pitch black and there's not a person in sight. I can't believe that Romeo would put me in danger just because he's angry.

After what seems like forever, Gwen and Elder LeRon pull up in his car. I only feel relieved for a second, because as soon as Gwen jumps out of the car, I know that I'm dead meat. Literally.

"Girl, what are you waiting on? Get in this car!" Gwen yells at the top of her lungs.

Quickly, I wipe the tears from my face and run over to the car. Gwen looks at me, pokes her lips out, and says, "Ain't no use in crying now!"

Elder LeRon says, "Calm down, Gwen. Let's just be happy that she's safe."

"Right. She is safe," Gwen says. "But she might not live to see her next birthday."

"You're overreacting," Elder LeRon says.

Gwen looks at him with a you-betta-mind-your-bidness-before-you-get-hurt-too glare and he backs all the way off. I close my eyes and lean my head against the backseat. I hope Elder LeRon takes the looooong way home, because once Gwen gets me alone, it's over.

My cell phone rings. I look down at the caller ID. It's Valerie. I hesitate before answering it, but Gwen is looking me dead in the face.

"Answer it," she says. "It might be the last phone call you get for a long time."

"Hello," I say into the phone.

Valerie asks, "Girl, did you call me earlier?"

"Yes."

"I was on the dance floor," she says. "This party is off the chain!"

"Glad to hear it."

Valerie laughs. "What is wrong with you? Where's Romeo?"

"He left me at the lake."

"Ooh, for real? That was dirty! Why'd you go to the lake with him? Only freaks go to the lake with boys."

Gwen gives me an evil glance that lets me know my one phone call is about done.

"Right, right," I say. "Valerie, I'm gonna have to let you go."

"Are you cool? Do you need me to come scoop you?"

"Nah. See you at school on Monday."

That's wishful thinking on my part. I hope I see Valerie on Monday. I hope I see tomorrow.

Much too quickly for my liking, Elder LeRon pulls up to our house. Gwen immediately gets out on her side, not even waiting for Elder LeRon to open the door. She storms up our walkway with me and Elder LeRon following far behind.

Gwen is trying to unlock the door when Elder LeRon touches her on the back. She jumps and turns to him with a frown. "Yes?" she asks.

"Do you need anything, Gwen? Would you like me to stay awhile?"

Clearly, Elder LeRon thinks my life is in danger. He would be correct. But that's cool of him to try and save me.

Gwen replies, "No, LeRon. This is something I have to handle alone as a parent. Thanks anyway."

Gwen finally gets the door unlocked and walks inside. Elder LeRon looks at me somewhat sympathetically and pats me on the back before going back to his car. I want to scream, *Take me with you!*

Instead, I walk in behind Gwen with my head down. Since I'm already in prayer position, I send a silent one up. *Dear Lord, please don't let Gwen kill me or worse, ground me for the rest of my life. I'm so sorry I was stupid and I'm sorry that I lied.*

"What do you have to say for your foolish self?" Gwen asks.

"Nothing."

Gwen laughs. It is an evil laugh. Then she says, "Oh, how can you have nothing to say? I want to hear all about your evening, and how your lying self ended up stranded at the beach looking like a fool."

The tears start down my face again. I've never seen Gwen this mad. Not even when I sneaked her gold earrings out of the house and lost them. Not even when I got really angry and called her a bad name.

"Now you're crying?" she asks. "You weren't crying when you were fixing your mouth to lie to me."

"I'm sorry, Mommy."

"Don't even, Gia. Don't. What happened to your little

boyfriend? He's the one who took you out to the lake, right?"

"He's not my boyfriend," I say truthfully.

"He's not? Well, he's somebody if he had your little silly self lying to me. Why did he leave your behind at the lake?"

"B-because, he was trying to touch on me, a-and I wouldn't l-let him."

Gwen sighs. "Well, at least you had that much sense."

Gwen paces the floor, back and forth. I guess she's trying to decide what to do to me. She seems to have calmed down a little bit. Maybe she's happy to know that I'm not a freak.

I shift my weight from one leg to another. I wish I had sat down on the couch while I had the chance. Now, I'm afraid to move.

After a long silence, Gwen says, "Lying to me is completely unacceptable."

"But I knew you'd never let me go out on a date," I try to explain. "I just want to be normal."

Gwen shakes her head angrily. "Little boys like Romeo are the reason I don't let you date. These boys out here are getting worse and worse."

"But I didn't know—"

Gwen cuts me off. "Of course you didn't know. You didn't know because you're young and naive. I knew as soon as I looked at his little sneaky behind what he was up to."

"Valerie said he liked me."

Gwen narrows her eyes and shakes her head. "Why do

you keep talking, Gia? You're not helping yourself. That heifer Valerie is another one! Got you wearing these ridiculous hairstyles and makeup. You look like a street-walker. Go wipe that mess off your face right now!"

Gwen looks like she's about to swing on me, so I make a mad dash for the bathroom. I see my reflection in the cracked mirror. I look a mess. Mascara and eyeliner are streaked beneath my eyes, giving me the raccoon look. My eyes and nose are puffy and red from crying.

I take a washcloth, soaked with warm water, and wipe the makeup from my eyes. When I'm done with this, I unclip the synthetic ponytail from my head and loosen my Afro so that it falls free. Now, I look more like my-self.

Gwen pops her head inside the bathroom. "Get on back out here and sit down on the couch."

I do as I'm told while Gwen pours herself a glass of Kool-Aid. She takes a long gulp and clears her throat. Here it comes.

"Gia, I think you need some time to think and pull yourself together. So, it's best if you turn in your Hi-Steppers uniform. . . ."

"Mama, no! I worked so hard for that!" I object.

Gwen is completely unaffected by my tearful words. "Yes, you did. But I worked hard to raise you not to be a liar."

I drop my head and watch the tears fall into my lap.

Gwen continues, "You will go to school and come straight home every day. You'll go to youth prayer, Bible study, and choir rehearsal. Your weekends will consist of working for Mother Cranford and bringing your behind home."

"For how long?" I ask.

"Until I believe you have good sense. And it won't be anytime soon. Now get out of my sight."

I run into my bedroom and hurl myself onto my bed. The tears keep coming as I bury my face into the pillow. My telephone buzzes on my hip.

"Hello," I say sadly, without even looking at the caller ID.

"Gia, it's me, Valerie. Are you okay? You sounded a little stressed earlier."

I clear my throat to try and hide that I've been crying. "I'm good. Everything's cool."

"So who came and picked you up? Was it Rick?" she asks.

"Don't even worry about it."

I'm about to hang up the phone when I hear Romeo's voice. "Man, why you on the phone with that lame?"

Wow on top of wow. So Romeo ditches me at the lake, where I could've gotten killed, and goes to party with Valerie. Just when I think it can't get any worse, it gets even crazier.

Next I hear Valerie's voice again. "Don't worry about him, Gia. He's just a little salty. He called Brad when he left you and Brad told him to come here."

"Mmm-hmm . . ."

"You don't think I'd leave you out there like that, do you? I totally had your back."

I press "end" on the phone because I can't stand to hear

Valerie's voice for another second. Maybe I would've believed she had my back if she wasn't giggling between every other word.

Gwen bursts into my room and says, "And hand me that phone, too. There's nobody you need to talk to but me."

★ 18 ★

Today is Sunday, the day after the last day of my life. I'm sitting in a pew at church, but I don't feel much like praising the Lord. My eyes are puffy and red from crying all night, and since I tossed Valerie's ponytail in the trash, my afro puff is back in full effect.

Looks like I'm back to my former lame self.

That's right. The lame chick that none of the boys were checking for. Except Kevin, and he doesn't count because he hasn't been confirmed to be an actual human.

Hope, who's serving as a junior usher today, hands me a church program. She takes a hard look at my face, then leans over and whispers, "What's up with you? You okay?"

I roll my eyes and fan myself with the program. Like she actually cares if I'm okay. She just wants to know what went down with Romeo. She'll have to hear about it from her mother, because trust and believe Gwen is going to call Pastor Stokes if she hasn't done it already.

"Forget you then, Gia. You're so evil."

Hope marches on up the aisle and hands out the rest of the programs. I don't care if she thinks I'm evil. Now she knows how I feel when I'm trying to deal with her.

Gwen is singing with the praise team this morning, and she keeps glaring over at me, like I'm about to pull off some caper up in the church. Shoot, my Bonnie and Clyde days are done. I'm not even thinking about doing anything shady.

Now here comes Ricky sliding himself down the pew. Gwen frowns even harder, but I act like I don't see her. Ricky has an apologetic look on his face, but I'm not in a forgiving mood.

He whispers, "Gia, I'm so sorry about last night."

"It's cool, Ricky."

"So did Gwen go crazy with the punishment?"

I chuckle sadly. "I may never see the light of day again."

"That bad, huh?"

I nod. "She's making me quit Hi-Steppers."

"For real?"

"Yeah."

Mother Cranford turns around in her seat the best she can, and says, "*Some* of us are trying to enjoy the service."

"We're sorry, Mother," Ricky says. I just look straight ahead, because Mother Cranford has been tripping on me since yesterday.

Ricky then whispers in my ear, "We'll talk after service."

Umm . . . yeah . . . no. Not talking to him either. Why is it that everyone wants to rehash my misery? Thank you very much, but I'll deal with this on my own. I don't need Hope's fake sympathy or Ricky's pity today.

Pastor Stokes preaches a message about Dinah. Yeah, she's a biblical character. She was one of Jacob's daughters, who was kicking it with this guy named Shechem, who wasn't one of God's people. Anyway, her brothers caught wind of it and ended up killing Shechem, his family, and his whole crew. And the Lord was not pleased.

Hmm . . . I wonder if my uncle is trying to tell me something.

Or maybe God is trying to tell me something.

Okay, I get it. Romeo was not the one I should've been dating. His name should've tipped me off. Do you know of any nice guys named Romeo? Well, except for that Shakespeare dude.

But just because Romeo wasn't the one, does that mean I'm supposed to stay in "my league" and fool with guys like Kevin. If that's the case, it's so not fair. I will never date Kevin. He is the opposite of everything I call fabulous.

After church is over, Gwen walks out of the choir stand and over to me. She says, "I'm going out to dinner after service. Elder LeRon is taking me."

"Am I going too?"

Gwen laughs. "No, sweetie. You are going straight to the house."

Ooh! This is so not right. "So what am I supposed to eat?"

"Bread and water. You might as well eat what jailbirds eat, because that's where all that lying is going to get you."

"Ma!"

Gwen sucks her teeth and shakes her head. "There's some spaghetti in the fridge. You can heat it up."

"Well, how am I getting home?" I ask. "Are you dropping me off?"

"No. Your uncle is. You can just have yourself a seat on this front pew until he gets done with the church business."

I sit on the pew and look around the church for my uncle. He's standing near his office door talking to the head of the nurses, Mother Billingsley. That conversation is going to take all day. She's probably giving him the rundown on her list of suspected sinners.

Aunt Elena sits next to me and puts her expensive hat into its hat box. She pats me on the back and says, "How are you doing, Gia? Is everything all right with you?"

Right. So, Gwen has already called my uncle. I guess they just all put their heads together and planned an intervention. Wow to infinity.

"I'm fine, Auntie. Thank you for asking."

"You know," she says, "I was thinking that maybe you'd like to have a girls' day with me and Hope this coming Saturday."

I think I just threw up in my mouth. I reply, "I work at Mother Cranford's on the weekends."

She shakes her head. "I can't believe Gwen has you working. Isn't school enough?"

I ignore this jab at my mother, because she's not my favorite person right now. Normally, I would remind my aunt that the Pastor's Aid Committee is not going to be footing the bill for my college education and so any extra money will help. But today, I'm not going there.

"I like working for Mother Cranford," I reply.

"Well, you could come over afterward and we could have a little spa party. We can give each other manis and pedis. It'll be fun." She scrunches up her nose when she says this. I guess the scrunching means it's gonna be *extra* fun.

I scrunch my nose right back. "Maybe."

I almost said I would ask Gwen, but that would be a lie. Since I'm sitting up in the sanctuary and all, I'm not trying to add any additional sins to my list.

"Well, you let me know when you're ready, Gia," my aunt says with the phoniest smile ever. "I would love to help make a lady out of you."

She wants to make a *lady* out of me! And the insults just keep on coming. Fortunately for Aunt Elena, Pastor Stokes walks up and he's got his coat on. That must mean it's time to leave. Finally!

We all pile into their car. Hope and I sit in the backseat. Since I don't want to have a conversation with her, I turn to stare out the window.

As Pastor Stokes drives out of the parking lot, Hope says, "Daddy, that was a good message today."

"Thank you, sweetie."

Hope continues, "It just shows how God is not pleased when you choose unsaved people as your friends."

Wow! I know Hope is not talking. She won't even talk to church members at school much less be friends with them. She's just trying to start a conversation about me and Romeo.

Pastor Stokes replies, "There's nothing wrong with being friendly to those outside the church. You are being a good witness for Christ when you show kindness to others."

"You're so right, Daddy," Hope says. "But you shouldn't have them for your boyfriend or anything. That's what Dinah did wrong."

Pastor Stokes clears his throat and sighs. Obviously, he sees what Hope is trying to do. I think sometimes he's embarrassed about how his wife and daughter treat me and Gwen.

He responds, "Why don't we just have some quiet time now, and reflect on the message, okay?"

"Okay, Daddy," Hope says. I don't look over at her, but I bet she's smirking at me.

When we get to my house, my uncle/pastor walks me up to the door. While I'm unlocking the door, he says, "Gia, your mom told me what happened with that boy."

"She did?" I ask as if I didn't already know.

"She was really worried, you know. She was at the church in tears."

I open the front door and say, "Thanks for making me feel even guiltier about it."

"Gwen only wants the best for you," he continues. "She wants you to have a better life than she did."

"I'm not her. I'm not *her*!" How many times do I have to say this? Does anybody even listen when I open my mouth?

"This is how it all started with Gwen. Our mother and father wouldn't let her go out on dates so she started sneaking out."

I can't imagine Gwen creeping. With all of her Bible

carrying, evangelizing, and prayer groups, it seems almost impossible. But I know it's true, because that's how I got here.

I reply, "I'm not going to lie anymore, Pastor, and no more boys will be asking me out."

"You know you can talk to me anytime, right? About anything. Boys, sex . . . anything."

"Okay."

My uncle then gives me a tight hug and kisses my forehead. "See you later, crocodile."

"Bye, alligator."

I turn and rush inside before anyone, especially Hope, sees the tears in my eyes.

★19★

This morning, before I left for school, I folded my Hi-Steppers uniform neatly and put it in a bag. The boots went on top, right along with my brand-new fabulous life. My sophomore year in high school is officially over.

Instead of the sparkly jeans and tight sweater, it's back to my favorite black Tweety T-shirt and normal jeans. That synthetic ponytail is in the trash can too. It's the old me back in full effect.

When I get to school, I walk into Mrs. Vaughn's office before I go to class. Sadly, I sit the brown paper bag with my uniform in it on her desk.

"What's this?" she asks.

I reply, "I have to quit the squad, Mrs. Vaughn."

"But why? You're one of the best choreographers we've got. We need you to help choreograph the televised game."

I swallow hard and reply, "I'm sorry, ma'am. My mother says I have to quit."

"Does she know how good Hi-Steppers would look on your college applications?"

"Yes, ma'am. Maybe she'll let me join next year."

Mrs. Vaughn asks, "Do you want me to give her a call?"

"No. It won't do any good, but thank you."

As I walk out of Mrs. Vaughn's office and down the hall to class, I see Valerie at her locker. And no this heifer does not have the audacity to look at me and smile. Does she honestly think we're still cool?

"Ooo-OOO! What's up, Hi-Stepper?" she screams down the hall.

I walk up on Valerie, straight gangsta style, and say, "Did you tell Romeo that I would give him some?"

"Girl, you better simmer down with all that action," Valerie says. "I know you don't think you can step to this!"

"You heard what I said, Valerie. Did you or did you not tell Romeo that I would give him some?"

Valerie laughs. "Give him some what, Gia? Are we in the third grade?"

"He said you told him I was down."

"Well, I didn't! I thought he liked you, but obviously he didn't if he played you like he did."

Since I don't have any proof that Valerie said anything to Romeo, I can't really accuse her of anything. All I have is his word, which isn't too reliable.

I reply, "Well, you can keep your ooo-OOO's to yourself, because I quit the squad."

"Wow," Valerie says with a smirk. "We're gonna miss you."

Somehow I don't think she's sincere.

I roll my eyes and walk down the hall to my first period class. It's French, and yeah, Romeo's in there. I wish I didn't have to see him this early in the morning.

I try to step into the classroom without anyone noticing me. It's harder than I hoped because Romeo's friend James is looking at me dead in my face, almost like he was waiting for me.

"Yo, Romeo. Look, it's your friend Blow Pop."

Even though I'd love to get into a ranking battle with James (he'd never win), I don't respond to him. I'm sure half the school already knows how Romeo played me, so I'm just trying to keep a low profile.

Romeo laughs out loud when he sees me. "Yeah, that's a good name for her. *Blow* Pop," he says with a smirk.

I look back at him with fire in my eyes. I know this fool is not gonna sit up here and act like I did anything nasty to him. If only I could turn back time. I'd go back and never give Romeo any shine.

A girl named Angela says, "Why were you even messing with a lame like her? Look at her clothes. Ewww!"

Just as I feel the tears try to come, Ms. Leiman shouts, "*Fermez votre bouches!*"

That means close your mouths. Never before have I been so happy to hear Ms. Leiman's crackly voice. She just said the sweetest words I've ever heard.

Then Romeo raises his hand and says, "Can I sharpenez my pencilez?"

"Mon dieu!" Ms. Leiman replies. She shakes her head in disgust at Romeo's butchering of the French language.

Romeo makes his way up my aisle. He pauses briefly at my desk and knocks my book to the floor. Everyone laughs.

I bite my bottom lip and look straight ahead. I can do this. I am strong enough to do this.

Then James screams from the back of the room, "How was the beach, Gia?"

Okay, so I lied. I can't do this.

I jump up from my seat, grab my bag and book from the floor and run out of the classroom. I want to leave school altogether, but if Gwen found out . . . I don't even want to think about what would happen if she did.

The first hiding place I see is the girls bathroom. I go into the last stall and hang my stuff on the door hook. Since I don't want anyone to know I'm here, I step onto the toilet seat and sit down on the top. Maybe now I can think.

All I wanted was to be popular, and have a cool guy think that I'm pretty. Now, Romeo's got me looking like I'm some kind of skank. Once that kind of thing gets around, it's over.

Maybe Gwen will let me switch schools.

Someone opens the bathroom door and I crouch down and try to make myself invisible. As soon as I hear the voices I almost let out a groan. It's Valerie and her drones, Jewel and Kelani.

Jewel asks, "Did y'all hear about Gia?"

"What about her?" Valerie says. She already knows what happened with me and Romeo, so why is she playing stupid?

"I heard that she and Romeo got busy out at Mentor Headlands," Kelani says.

There is a moment of silence, and then Valerie says, "It's not true. She didn't give him any."

What? Is Valerie actually defending me? There may be some hope for my popularity after all.

"Well, that's what Romeo is saying," Jewel replies.

"I know what he's saying," Valerie counters, "but he's lying. This was not how it was supposed to go down."

Kelani asks the question that I'm thinking, "How *what* was supposed to go down?"

Valerie laughs. "Romeo was just supposed to keep Gia out of my way so that I could go after Rick. He wasn't supposed to play her like this. He's out of control."

"Why would he help you hook up with Rick?" Jewel asks.

"I've got dirt on Romeo that could get him thrown off the football team."

"Oh," Kelani asks. "That explains it."

"Enough about that. How does my booty look in these jeans?" Jewel asks.

Valerie replies, "Girl, it's on swole, for real. Let's go, before the security guards come up in here."

They walk out of the bathroom and leave me sitting here feeling heated. All of this—the makeover, Romeo pretending like he wanted me—was actually for Valerie? Because she wanted me out of her way?

But why did she even care about me? Me and Ricky are not a couple. Basically, she's destroyed my life for nothing.

I am so not about to let this go.

★20★

"**W**hat's the matter, Gia?"

I look up at Gwen from my spot on the living room floor. I'm sitting here crossed-legged, trying to figure out how to get back at Valerie, but I'm coming up empty.

"Nothing."

"It sure doesn't look like nothing!" Gwen says. "You're over there looking like you're mad at the world."

Not mad at the world, just Valerie.

I should be at Hi-Steppers practice choreographing a fly routine for the Homecoming game. That's when the cameras are going to be there and our game will be on public access television and the evening news.

It's gonna be so fresh, but instead I will be chilling here at the house with Gwen. We'll probably make some popcorn and watch Lifetime movies. Or even better, maybe we'll fast and pray. Yippie.

Then Saturday night, everybody's going to be at the Homecoming dance. I thought I was gonna be going with Romeo, maybe a double date with Ricky and Valerie. It feels like it was so long ago that I was almost popular. But I guess what they say is true . . . "almost" really *doesn't* count.

Gwen says, "Ricky told me that he might get to play in the Homecoming game."

"Yeah, he probably will," I reply. "They're playing the Normandy Eagles, and that's always an easy game. I won't be there to see it, so I really don't care."

Gwen clears her throat and sighs like maybe she's feeling sorry for me. She motions for me to move over to the table. "Come here, Gia. Sit down."

I look at the spread of beauty supply products on the table. "Are you about to comb my hair?"

"Yes. Do you have a problem with it?" Gwen asks with a smile.

"No, but you haven't done my hair in a long time."

She pats the seat of the wooden chair. "Come on."

First, Gwen takes down my afro puff and separates my hair into four sections. She puts a coconut-scented cream in each section and combs through it with a huge wide-toothed comb. Then she puts the back two sections into rubber bands and parts the front with a rat-tailed comb.

I relax in the chair as Gwen puts tiny crisscrossed cornrows all over the front of my head. She connects them together into one big braided band across my head and then pics out the back into a big curly fro.

When she's done, my mother hands me a mirror so

that I can see her creation. Surprisingly, it's fly! It's much cuter than that fake ponytail Valerie had me rocking. I smile at myself.

"Mom, this looks fresh! Thank you."

Gwen is pleased. "It is fresh, isn't it?"

I could see me wearing this hairstyle with my glitter Tweety T-shirt and a jean skirt. I wonder if I could learn to do this myself. Maybe I could even put a little flower behind my ear too, like Mother Cranford.

"So," Gwen says, "I was thinking that maybe I'd let you go to the Homecoming game to cheer Ricky on."

I give Gwen a hug. "Thank you, Mommy!"

"I was thinking maybe we'd go together," Gwen says.

I narrow my eyes suspiciously. "You want to go to a football game with me?"

"Sure! You are my daughter, right?"

"Wait a minute," I say. "Is Elder LeRon coming?"

"Nope. It's just gonna be you and me."

Since she's in a good mood, I might as well go for it all. "Can I go to the Homecoming dance too?"

"You are still on punishment, boo," Gwen says with her hands on her hips. "Don't try to play me."

"Okay, Mom."

I walk into youth choir rehearsal, rocking my new hairstyle. Guess who notices first? That's right. Mr. Saved-and-Sanctified-Kevin.

I'm feeling good about still getting to go to the Homecoming game, even if I won't be marching with the Hi-Steppers. So Kevin can't even get on my nerves this evening.

"Praise the Lord, Gia!" he says. Dude is way too excited.

"Hey, Kev. What it do?"

He looks puzzled. "What does what do?"

"Never mind."

"Your hair is pretty," Kevin comments.

"Thanks."

I sashay myself on up to the choir stand right past Brother Bryan. And did I see him do a double take? Ha! I wish. Sister Regina just walked into the sanctuary wearing a tight skirt.

I take my place between Hope and Ricky on the border of the soprano and tenor sections. Ricky looks happy to see me, although we haven't had words since Sunday at church. I've been avoiding him at school along with everyone else.

"Why didn't you answer my text?" Ricky asks in a whisper.

"Dude. Punishment? Gwen yanked my cell phone."

Ricky nods. "Okay, but Kevin and I haven't seen you in the cafeteria at lunch time either."

"I had a history paper due. Been in the library during lunch."

I don't think Ricky believes my excuses, but I'm off the hook because Brother Bryan is starting rehearsal. Ricky folds his arms and frowns at me, like he intends on interrogating me more later. Whatev.

"All right, y'all. We're singing this Sunday, so let's get this harmony part right: And His name is Jesus. On three. One . . . two . . . three . . ."

The whole choir sings, "And His name is Jesus!"

Brother Bryan waves his hand at the musicians to tell them to stop playing. "One of the tenors is off. Is that you, Ricardo?"

Everybody laughs. Ricky replies, "I don't think so."

"Well, let me hear it: And His name is Jesus!"

"And His name is Jesus!" Ricky sings perfectly in tune.

Brother Bryan smiles. "Well, you've got that down. Let's see if you can get that pass down on Friday night. We want to see a Longfellow victory, right, y'all?"

Everyone in the choir stand applauds and shouts. Brother Bryan used to play for Longfellow when he was in high school. He was the starting quarterback during his senior year and landed a full ride to Grambling State. So, to say the least, he is a huge Longfellow Spartans fan.

After rehearsal, everyone is at the back of the church talking about Homecoming. Hope asks Ricky, "Are you taking Valerie to Homecoming?"

Ricky looks at the ground. "Nah. I haven't asked her yet, so it's probably too late."

Although I'm nowhere near being a part of this conversation, Kevin tries to rope me in. He asks, "What about you, Gia? Do you want to go with me?"

"Oh, Kevin. I wish I could, but I'm on punishment."
Thank you, Jesus! Please be a punishment fence all around me everyday!

Kevin looks sad. "That's too bad. My grandfather was going to drop us off in his Cadillac."

That is so not funny. Kevin's grandfather's Cadillac is a

big-bodied 1978 Eldorado. And no it does not have rims, spinners, or anything fly. It does have a nice layer of rust, though. Ewwww!!!

Ricky asks me, "Is your mom gonna let you go to the game, at least?"

"Yep. She's coming too."

"Cool."

I guess this breaks the ice between me and Ricky, because he pulls me away from the group. He asks in a low voice, "Do you need me to handle Romeo? He's talking real reckless right about now."

"Handle him? What do you mean, fight him like the last time?"

"Well, yeah."

I punch Ricky in the arm. "Don't be stupid. You're about to get some playing time on Friday. I don't want you to get suspended."

"So what do you want to do?"

The more I think about it, I have a bigger problem with Valerie than I do with Romeo. I mean, Romeo is who he is. I've seen him play lots of girls. I've even laughed at some of them. I don't know why I thought I'd be any different.

But Valerie pretended to be my friend, just so she could get to Ricky. She gave me a makeover and hooked me up with a boy who would hurt me, just so she could get me out of the way. And she doesn't even like Ricky! She's playing him with that lame Brad.

I look up at Ricky and reply, "My beef is more with Valerie than Romeo."

"You don't have to worry about beef, Gia. The Lord will handle it," Ricky says.

I keep the next thought to myself. That the popular and pretty people like Valerie and Romeo never seem to pay for what they do. It sure would be nice to get a little revenge.

★ 21 ★

It's Wednesday, two days before the Homecoming game. As I walk down the hallway to my locker, Jewel and Kelani stand by the wall glaring at me. So not in the mood for their foolishness, I ignore them.

But they don't seem to want to let me get away. Jewel says, "You're foul for quitting the Hi-Steppers squad right before the Homecoming game. You know we're gonna be on TV."

"Yeah, we needed you for choreography," Kelani adds.

I don't know how to reply because they actually sound sad. So, I try to explain. "I didn't want to quit the squad. I'm on punishment."

Jewel replies, "Well, then your mother is foul."

Usually, I don't let anyone get away with saying anything about Gwen, but in this case, Jewel might be right. It's not really fair that the rest of the Hi-Steppers have to pay for my lies.

Since I stopped to talk to those two, I'm running late for my second period geometry class. If I don't make it by the bell, I will mos def have a detention because Mr. Asamoto doesn't play.

I slam my locker shut and get ready to sprint in the direction of my classroom when someone taps me on the shoulder. I turn around and it's Coach Rogers—the football coach.

"Ms. Stokes, will you come to my office right now, please?"

"Coach Rogers, I've got geometry this period."

"I'll write you a note. This is important."

Coach Rogers is strangely quiet as we walk to his office, so my mind is forced to wander. What does he want with me? I hope this doesn't have anything to do with that fight between Romeo and Ricky, because I really want Ricky to get some playing time on Friday.

"Am I in trouble?" I ask.

Coach Rogers smiles. "No, you're not in trouble. It sounds like you've already been through enough."

Now I'm really confused. What is he talking about? I mean, you know and I know that I've been through quite a bit. But what does Coach Rogers know? I didn't think that the teachers got in on the school gossip too.

Finally, we get to Coach Rogers's office. It's connected to the huge sports equipment room. I gasp as we walk through the office door, because Romeo and his fly mama are sitting at the desk. Romeo's mother rolls her eyes at me and pokes out her glossy and glittered fuchsia-colored lips. Out in the equipment room, the entire football team is lined up. Ricky is front and center, and he's grinning at me.

Suddenly Romeo's mother shouts, "Mmm-hmm! This is the little heifer that tried to seduce my son!"

"Ma, can you please be quiet?" Romeo pleads.

Coach Rogers says, "Mrs. Washington, we're going to get to the bottom of this, right now."

"How? By asking this little hoochie mama some questions? She ain't gonna do nothin' but lie!"

Why does this woman look me up and down like she's about to fight me? I do not put it past her, so I take two steps closer to Coach Rogers in case she takes a swing at me.

I close my eyes and shake my head in disbelief. This is crazy with a capital CRAZY! Why is this woman trying to destroy me even further? Her son already has me looking like his freak of the week.

Coach Rogers turns to me and asks, "Gia, is it true that Romeo took you out to the lake and left you stranded there?"

I nod slowly while giving Romeo's mama some serious side eye. She better not try to touch me with those airbrushed acrylic nails. In case you care, she happens to be wearing Apple Bottoms jeans and boots with the fur. . . .

"Girl, bye!" Romeo's mother shouts. "You know that's a lie. My son told me he took her out on a date and she tried to sexually assault him. My son is a perfect gentleman."

Coach Rogers replies, "I would find it much easier to believe Romeo if I hadn't heard him in the locker room bragging about this, Mrs. Washington."

Romeo's mother looks at him, sucks her teeth and then slaps him in the back of the head. "Boy, you so stupid. I thought I taught you better than that!"

Some of the football players laugh, but Coach Rogers shuts that down real quick with one glance. He then says, "Romeo, I'm going to give you some choices. These choices will help you determine whether or not you want to remain a Longfellow Spartan."

"Yes, sir," Romeo says.

Coach Rogers continues, "You can apologize to Ms. Stokes in front of your teammates, whom you've also offended with your character."

"My son is not apologizing to her! She needs to be apologizing to him. As a matter of fact, she needs to be thanking him for asking her out, because my son doesn't date busted girls!" Romeo's mother exclaims.

Coach Rogers ignores her. "Or, you can not apologize, stay cool, and swagger yourself out of this locker room and off this team."

Romeo looks up at Coach Rogers, to his teammates, and then at me. He has tears in his eyes, but I don't know if they mean that he's sorry for how he treated me or just that he's embarrassed.

Then he says in a very, very small voice, "I'm sorry."

"Romeo, if you're going to apologize, you're going to do it like a man," Coach Rogers says. "Stand up and address this young lady."

Romeo stands and looks directly into my eyes. "Gia, I apologize for taking you out to the lake and leaving you there. I'm sorry for trying to make you do something you didn't want to do, and I'm sorry for spreading lies about you."

"I forgive you, Romeo," I reply.

"Thank you, Gia. You can go to class now," Coach Rogers says as he hands me a hall pass.

As I walk out of Coach Rogers's office, a smile spreads across my face. I can't help it. My first date might have been a disaster, but having Romeo apologize to me in front of the entire team is priceless.

After school, I head straight over to Mother Cranford's house. She can't wreck my mood today, no matter what slave labor she plans on giving me.

When I get to her house, guess who's already standing on her porch? It's Ricky, Hope, and Kevin.

"What are y'all doing here?" I ask.

Ricky says, "We knew you had to work today, and since Sister Gwen has you on lockdown, we decided to hang out here."

Okay, I get Ricky and Kevin wanting to hang out with me. But Hope? Yeah, not so much. I raise one eyebrow at her and wait for her explanation.

"Do I need permission to hang with my cousin?" she asks innocently.

Now Kevin and Ricky look at Hope with questions in their eyes. She throws one hand up and sighs. "All right! Valerie and her crew are starting to irk me. I just wanted to hang with you guys."

"Did you just come here to ask me what went down with Romeo?" I ask.

Hope puts one hand on her hip. "No! I didn't have to ask you about that because everyone already knows! I heard Coach Rogers made Romeo get down on one knee and apologize."

Ricky, Kevin, and I burst into laughter. "That did not happen," I say.

"He should've gotten down on one knee," Ricky says.

"It's cool if y'all hang with me," I decide. "But I don't know how Mother Cranford is going to feel about all this company."

As if on cue, Mother Cranford swings open her door and says, "Are y'all gonna stand out here all afternoon?"

We all pile into Mother Cranford's house. I go straight to the kitchen to get her evening snack. Ricky and Kevin set up shop near Mother Cranford's recliner so they can watch TV with her, and Hope plops down on the comfortable sofa and opens a novel.

Mother Cranford says, "Well, I ain't had this much company since I was still baking pound cakes every week."

"Did someone say cake?" Hope asks.

Ricky laughs and says, "Mother, we love visiting with you."

"You are such a *nice* young man," Mother Cranford says. "You and this brother Kevin."

"What about me?" I ask. Shoot! I'm the one who has been high dusting and all this other foolishness, and at slave wages.

"You started out all right, till you started smellin' yourself."

Hope, Kevin, and Ricky all burst out laughing. Excuse me! "Smellin' myself"? If Mother Cranford wasn't almost a hundred years old, I'd give her a big fat *Girl bye!*

"Mother, I don't know what you're talking about," I reply. "I am definitely not smelling myself, and if I did smell myself it would be fresh and clean!"

This, of course, brings out more laughter from the giggle posse. Mother Cranford counters, "Baby, it's a good thang you took that little plastic ponytail out your head because you was lookin' right foolish."

Is Mother Cranford ranking me? Would the Lord be pleased about me having a ranking contest with a church mother? Me thinks no.

Kevin adds his little two cents. "Yeah, Gia. I like your real hair better."

"Me too," Ricky says.

"Hey, hold up! What's with the triple team?"

Hope clears her throat and says, "While I am not fond of that little puffy thing, that synthetic ponytail was *not* the business."

I drop my dust cloth on the floor and look from Mother Cranford, to Ricky, to Kevin, and then to Hope. "So none of y'all liked my ponytail? Why didn't you say something?"

Ricky replies, "Because you liked it, and friends support one another."

Mother Cranford smiles. "See, girl, these here are the ones who care about you. That silly heifer who came to pick you up and was honking like she didn't have good sense—she ain't your friend."

"You betta' preach, Mother!" Hope says. "Valerie isn't anyone's friend."

Ricky changes the subject. "Mother Cranford, are you going to watch my game on TV Friday night? A lot of people from the church are coming."

"Is that right? Well, I don't know much about football, but I'd be happy to cheer you on."

Hope asks, "Gia, are you going to the game?"

"Yeah, me and Gwen are going."

"I was thinking that I might go with you guys."

Again, I'm shocked. "But what about the Hi-Steppers?"

Hope looks at the floor and says, "I found out some things about Valerie that I couldn't take, so I quit the squad."

It sounds like everybody is getting hip to Valerie and her shenanigans. It also sounds like maybe I've got my cousin back.

★ 22 ★

Have a good game ☺
That's the text I just sent Ricky. Hope, my mom, and I just got to the football field and we're walking up the stairs and into the stands. I'm rocking that glitter Tweety just like I said I would, with a little blue-jean skirt.

"You look cute," Hope says.

I look at her like she's crazy. Hope giving me compliments and hanging with me is just too weird.

Hope laughs. "You can say thank you."

"Who are you and what did you do with my cousin?" I ask.

"Gia, you are crazy."

The Hi-Steppers march past us clicking their white boots and yelling Ooo-OOO! Briefly, I make eye contact with Valerie, but she looks away quickly. I wonder if she feels guilty about helping Romeo play me.

I'm surprised when Jewel and Kelani wave at us. Maybe they're happy about being on TV tonight, or maybe we'll all end up being cool. I guess I just have to wait and see.

Gwen picks a bleacher and we all sit down. Then I continue with my questioning of Hope. "Real talk, Hope. I don't know how to take you being friendly all of a sudden."

"I want us to be friends again, Gia. Plus, it scared me when Romeo left you out at the lake that night. I got to thinking how awful it would be if something happened to you."

I blink a few times, not knowing how to respond to this. Fortunately, I don't have to respond because the game is starting. The cheerleaders, minus senior Kellie Johnson (she's Homecoming Queen), are starting their opening chant.

They shout, "One, we are the Spartans! Two, a little bit louder! Three, I still can't hear you! Four, more, more, more!"

Things are going well for the Spartans. Early in the game, Lance Rogers makes a thirty-yard pass to Romeo, who takes it into the end zone.

Everyone stands up and cheers, including Romeo's ghetto mama, who is sitting a few bleachers down from us. She stays rocking those Apple Bottoms jeans, but tonight she hit up the beauty supply store and cleaned them out of all the platinum-colored hair they had in stock. She's got about eighteen bulks of hair on her head and it's cascading halfway down her back.

Gwen whispers to me, "That woman looks a mess."

By halftime, the Spartans are winning thirty-five to seven,

but Ricky still isn't in the game. He'll probably start playing after the halftime show because Lance is Homecoming King.

Speaking of the Homecoming court, they are all prancing onto the field right now. No one in my limited circle even cares about Homecoming, but the cheerleader posse is very pumped with one of their own as the queen.

Hope and I watch as the Hi-Steppers line up with the band. It looks like Valerie is giving last minute instructions to the girls as they walk onto the field. The television camera crew is right on the edge of the field and they're set up to get a great shot of the Hi-Steppers squad.

As soon as the Homecoming court exits the field, the band and the Hi-Steppers start their show. I should probably feel bad about hoping that Valerie trips and falls and that her feet fly up in the air and her thong is exposed to the crowd. But somehow, I can't feel guilty.

Much to my disappointment, the Hi-Steppers are on point. Their step is a little on the lame side, which couldn't be helped since I was unavailable to choreograph the routine. Naturally, Valerie gives herself an extended solo where she gets low, low, low to the ground, which makes all of the boys cheer.

What a skank.

The second half of the football game is great! Ricky gets put in at the end of the third quarter and he throws three touchdown passes. The Longfellow Spartans crush the other team with a fifty-six to ten victory.

As we're walking out of the stands with the rest of the Spartans fans, Hope asks, "Auntie Gwen, can Gia and I pleeeeeease go to IHOP with the rest of the team? We've got to help Ricky celebrate!"

Gwen thinks for a moment, and then replies, "How about we *all* go to IHOP? I like pancakes."

"Auntie, no! We promise to only stay for a little while and we won't leave with any boys. Right, Gia?"

Wow. Why did I have to be included in this request? I would rather just go straight to the house and not have to ever see Romeo again.

But since Hope has roped me into this, I reply, "Mom, I do want to congratulate Ricky. And I promise that I won't do anything."

Gwen looks at both of us as if she's trying to figure out if we're up to something. If she only knew how far past scheming I am. I don't have another scheming or plotting bone in my body. A sista like me does not enjoy getting grounded.

Finally Gwen says, "All right, but you two better be hustling your behinds to the house in one hour. Got it?"

"Yes, Auntie!" Hope throws her arms around Gwen's neck and gives her a big, sloppy, wet kiss on the cheek.

Gwen looks completely uncomfortable with all this mushy affection. Me and Gwen don't do mushy.

As usual, IHOP is popping. All of the football players are here and so are the cheerleaders and Hi-Steppers. Actually, it's a much bigger crowd than usual, probably because it's Homecoming weekend.

"So where should we sit?" Hope asks.

Good question. Usually we sit with the Hi-Steppers,

but I'm not really feeling Valerie and I don't even know if we're still welcome. The cheerleaders would probably look at us like we're crazy if we try to take a seat at their table, and I'm not planning to be anywhere near Romeo and his posse.

"Why don't we sit at our own table?" I say.

"Cool."

Hope and I score a booth in the corner, and I look around for Ricky. Finally, I spot him and, of course, he's surrounded by some of his biggest fans.

"Look at them!" I complain to Hope. "Why are they on him like that? Them chicks is so thirsty!"

Hope follows my eyes to Ricky. "Yeah, they are thirsty, but you gotta admit, Rick is pretty hot."

"Umm . . . his name is Ricky or Ricardo if you're gonna use the name his mama gave him."

"Whatever!" Hope laughs.

But I'm not finished. I've got more questions. "And since when do you think Ricky is hot?"

A sly smile creeps up on Hope's face. "He's been a cutie for a minute. Don't act like you don't know."

Hope waves at one of her Hi-Stepper friends like she didn't just say something monumental. Me no likee.

When he's finished with his adoring fans, Ricky plops down at our table. Then he says, "Go ahead and congratulate me."

"Boy, you need to quit feeling yourself!" I exclaim. "I want to see you throw all those touchdown passes against a real team."

What? Somebody's got to bring him back down to planet Earth. And it might as well be me. If we don't intervene now, he might start referring to himself in the third person like someone else we know.

Hope gushes, "Ricky, you were the bomb tonight! I know you're gonna be a starter next year."

"Thanks, Hope! At least somebody over here is my friend."

Hope giggles. "That's right, Ricky. But don't worry about Gia. Haters gone hate!"

They both burst into giggles and I give both of them the hand. And no they are not trying to sit up here being all jokey jokey. Hope better simmer her little self on down, and Ricky already knows what it is.

Valerie sashays her narrow behind up to our booth and scoots in on Ricky's side. For a second, it looked like he wasn't going to let her in. Has my boy finally been freed of Valerie fever? Has the Lord finally answered one of my prayer requests?

"So, Rick," Valerie says, "you did your thang out there on the field tonight. I'm so proud to say that you're my boo."

Gag on top of gag on top of gag. Gag infinity. There are no limits to how much this chick disgusts me. And that's for real.

Ricky carefully removes the arm that Valerie has placed around his shoulder. Then he says, "Valerie, quit playing. I'm not your boo."

"Of course you are!" Valerie argues.

"That's not what my boy Brad said," Ricky replies bluntly.

He knows! Woo-hoo! I feel like breaking into one of Mother Cranford's Holy Ghost shouts. I'm sure there is an expression of glee on my face, because I feel myself grinning from ear to ear.

Valerie looks confused, and then she frowns over at me. "I don't know what you're talking about."

"Sure you do," Ricky says. "We were in study hall and Brad was telling everyone how you two are kicking it and going to his brother's party after Homecoming."

"T-that's not true," Valerie stutters.

Ricky replies, "Sorry, Valerie. I don't believe you. You need more people."

Valerie stands up and puts her hand on her hips. "Rick, you really should not listen to your little lame friends. Being my boo is the come-up of a lifetime for you. Don't forget you're just a second-string quarterback that used to have a severe acne problem."

"I haven't forgotten, and by the way, my name is Ricky. Run along to your Hi-Steppers. You're dismissed."

My mouth drops open and so does Hope's! No he didn't just dismiss Valerie and her booty from our table! I'm so proud of Ricky right now, I could just kiss him. Ahem . . . I mean I could give him a really friendly, sisterly hug.

Valerie laughs. "You can't dismiss me. You don't have the clout to dismiss me! *You* need more people, boo."

Valerie struts away from our booth, picking her face up off the floor as she goes. As soon as she's far enough away, we all burst into laughter.

I have to ask, "How long have you known about Brad?"

"For a while. It's cool, though. She isn't my type anyway," Ricky replies.

Hope smiles that weird smile again and asks, "What is your type, Ricky?"

OMG! Jesus take me. Take me now!

"Hope, we better get to the house before Gwen starts tripping," I say. It is time to break up this foolishness.

Ricky replies, "Cool. I can walk with y'all."

Sheesh! It looks like I'm gonna have to deal with Hope's goo-goo eyes all the way to the crib. But since the rest of the evening has gone so well, I guess I can deal.

On the way out of IHOP, one of the football players says, "Hey, you're lookin' fly with that afro puff, ma."

I stop and stare in amazement. First, because I'm trying to see if he's for real and not one of Romeo's goons looking to clown me. But the smile he's wearing is sincere, so I smile right back.

★ 23 ★

Ricky walks me and Hope back to my house when we leave IHOP. I must say that I'm feeling good for several reasons. First, Valerie and Romeo have been completely owned and I'm lovin' it. Romeo apologizing to me in front of the entire football team and his mama is like the highlight of my year.

I'm so glad that Ricky emerged from that Valerie-lovin' cocoon and told her to step. He deserves so much better than that. And not Hope either—she needs to fall back, on the real.

The second thing I'm psyched about is that I might not be invisible anymore. Y'all know how church people say, "All things work together for the good"? Well, that means when bad things happen to you, sometimes they can turn out to be good things.

I said all that because it's possible that this mess with Romeo might have made all this fabulosity that I've got going on obvious to the rest of the world. Anyway, that's what I'm hoping.

When we get to my house Ricky points at the car in the driveway. "Why is Elder LeRon here?"

"Yuck! I don't know! I wish he'd take himself on home. His presence is beyond irking."

Hope comments, "I think he's nice."

I ask Ricky, "Are you coming in to say hello to Gwen?"

"Of course. She'll fuss at me if I don't."

The three of us walk into the house to the sound of Gwen screaming. At first I'm alarmed, but then I realize she's doing her "filled with the Holy Ghost" shout and laughing all at the same time.

I ask, "What's going on up in here?"

"This!" Gwen squeals as she thrusts her hand into my face. "Elder LeRon and I are getting married!"

"Mama, no!"

Elder LeRon laughs. "Mama, yes! In six months, you're going to have a new family, including my fourteen-year-old daughter. You know Candy, right?"

I feel myself fainting and falling into Ricky's arms. Hush my mouth and clutch the pearls. Jesus, be a stepchild fence all around me. . . .

★ 24 ★

"**G**al, what has gotten into you today?" The sound of Mother Cranford's voice snaps me out of my daze. I'm still in a catatonic state of shock over Gwen and Elder LeRon's announcement. First of all, I was not consulted when this decision was made. Second of all, and more importantly, I do not want a younger sister.

"I'm sorry, Mother Cranford. Do you need something?" I ask apologetically.

Mother Cranford purses her lips together until they look like a thin slash of fire-engine red lipstick. Oh, yes, Mother rocks that red lipstick on the regular. I don't think I've ever seen her without it.

She replies, "I need you to bring your head out of the clouds and fix my lunch. Do you think you can accomplish that?"

Okay, today is truly not the day for her to start tripping. I'm having an emergency and Mother Cranford is the only person I've got to talk to. Ricky and Hope are both unavailable, because it's the night of the Homecoming dance. I've sent them both about a hundred text messages, and neither of them has responded. I have the best friends in the whole wide world.

Clearly, I'm being sarcastic.

I jump up from my spot on the floor and pop Mother Cranford's Lean Cuisine in the microwave. She eats these things like they're going out of style. You'd think that she'd be *leaner* since it's all she eats, but alas she is not. Mother must have a pack of Oreos in that purse she always holds on her lap.

"Are you going to answer my question?" Mother Cranford says.

"Which one?"

She clicks her tongue on the top of her dentures and it makes a loud popping noise. "What is the matter with you, girl? You are all out of sorts."

"Oh. That question. Well, my mother is getting married," I reply sadly.

Mother Cranford claps her hands and squeals. "Praise be to God! Who is the blessed fella?"

Blessed? That's a way of looking at it, I guess. We know that Elder LeRon is blessed to be getting my mother (even though she's irking, she's still fly), but are we blessed to be getting him?

"My mother is marrying Elder LeRon Ferguson."

"He is a good man. I remember him when he was a boy. Your granddaddy thought he was something special with that preaching and all."

"Elder LeRon went to Grandpa Stokes's church?"

"He sure did. Then he ran off when he was eighteen and married the first girl he fell for. Yes he did."

Wow, Mother Cranford knows everybody's business. What's up with that? I do love when she starts talking about my grandfather, though. I don't remember much about him, although everyone says I look a lot like him.

"I guess things didn't work out with his first wife," I say to Mother Cranford. "I wonder why she left him."

She frowns. "I do believe that's grown folk business. You don't need to be worrying about that."

"Sorry, Mother Cranford."

Then she leans in close and says, "But I heard she was messing with them drugs. He took that baby girl away from her until she got herself cleaned up."

Like I said, Mother Cranford knows everybody's business.

My cell phone rings. Finally! I thought everyone had forgotten about little old me.

"Talk to me," I say, after peeking at the caller ID and seeing that it's Hope.

"Gia, I'm not in the mood for your foolishness today."

I giggle and reply, "It's about time you called me back."

"Where's the fire? And you are straight tripping sending all those text messages. If I go over my limit for the month, Daddy is going to be salty."

"Enough about your issues! I've got a crisis over here."

Hope laughs. "Did you get a comb trapped in that afro puff?"

Umm . . . not laughing. Probably because I have broken several dollar store combs trying to tame the curlfro.

"Ha, ha. You are the opposite of funny," I point out. "The emergency is this nonsense about Gwen getting married."

"Nonsense? I think it's great, Gia. You need to get over yourself."

"Great? What's great about having to move out of my house to live with some strange man and his little irritating child? I see nothing great about it."

"Dang, Gia, tell me how you really feel," Hope says with a chuckle.

"I'm serious, Hope."

"Okay, okay. I understand why you might be worried, but Elder LeRon is cool people! Don't you want your mother to be happy?"

"Yes, I do. She deserves it."

"Well, then quit tripping and suck it up. Daddy is about to drive me and Ricky to the dance. Are you cool?"

"You and Ricky? What do you mean?"

"Fall back, little cousin. Me and Ricky aren't going as a couple. He just needed a ride."

"Oh, all right. I'm just making sure."

"Girl, please! I'll holla at you after the dance. Are you going to be awake?"

"Yep."

"All right then. Holla!"

I press the "end" button on my cell phone. It's cool that me and Hope are friends again. I didn't think it was possible. Actually, it was on my super long list of impossibilities. It was right up there with Ricky asking me to be his girlfriend.

Hmm . . . it could happen. Right?

★ 25 ★

While all of the cool people are chilling at the Homecoming dance, I'm being detained against my will. Gwen is forcing me to have dinner with her man and his little bratty daughter, Candy.

This is the opposite of fair. I would rather be doing almost anything but this. I would even rather be dancing with moist-hands Kevin at the Homecoming dance. Okay, maybe not, but it's still not fair.

I've met Candy before, at church, but I guess she lives with her mother because we only see her on the times when daddies get a visit—Christmas, Easter, and Father's Day. She's a couple of years younger than me and in the eighth grade.

Gwen's gone all out and cooked her best meal—spaghetti and meatballs. She even bought the loaf of crusty, gooey garlic bread that she never buys because it's not in the budget. She's sure trying to impress this man! I just hope he likes spaghetti and chicken because he's about to be eating a lot of it.

Mom steps out of her bedroom and asks, "How do I look?"

I look her up and down to see if I approve of her outfit. It's a dress that she bought on our last shopping expedition to TJ Maxx. The top is white and the bottom is black. It has a big black belt in the middle with a flower for the buckle. It's cute, even if it's a little on the short side.

Finally, I reply, "Umm . . . I don't think Pastor would approve of you showing off all your legs like that."

"Girl, I ain't thinking about my little brother! He ain't running nothing up in here."

"Wow, Sister Stokes, you are awfully rebellious, aren't you? The Lord is not pleased."

Gwen laughs. "It's about to be Sister Ferguson, wife of an elder in the church! Hallelujah to Jesus!"

Wow. She's about to get her shout on, right in the middle of our living room. What? You don't know what a shout is? Hmm . . . how do I explain? Well, it's when church people get so happy about what God has done for them that they just can't stay still. They've got to get up and move!

Gwen shouts about a lot of stuff, like having enough money to pay bills and being healthy and in her right mind (this is still up for discussion—I'm not sure she's in her right mind). But she's been waiting to shout about landing herself a husband ever since I was a little baby.

"Mom, if you start shouting, then you are going to have to change your clothes."

Gwen places her hand over her heart and breathes deeply. I guess she's trying to calm herself down. It seems to be working.

"God is just so good, baby. I just can't tell it."

Finally, we hear Elder LeRon's car pull up in the driveway. Gwen takes a last look around the house and straightens up the couch pillows. She sees a shoe sticking out from underneath the couch and throws that through her bedroom door. I'm just looking at her like she's crazy, because I've never seen her get this twisted over a man before.

"Open the door, Gia!" Gwen fusses as she starts carrying food into the dining room.

I swing the door open for Elder LeRon and Candy. They're standing outside on the walkway, and it looks like Elder LeRon is having a bit of a problem.

Elder LeRon says, "Candy, come on! I'm not joking with you."

"You can't make me go in there!" Candy shouts. "I don't want to meet your new lady friend!"

I have to cover my mouth to keep from giggling. Lady friend! Oh my goodness.

"Candy, I've already told you, Sister Gwen is my fiancée. She's not just a lady friend anymore."

Candy pouts and crosses her arms. Then she looks at me with a pleading expression on her face. "Will you please let me use a phone so I can call my mom?"

Now, why'd she have to go and put me in this mess? Plus, she's out there lightweight dogging my mother. Why should I help her?

"Umm . . . doesn't your dad have a phone?" I ask, tossing their little mess right back outside my door where it belongs.

Elder LeRon looks like he's about to explode. He's red in the face and his cheeks are all puffed out like he's a tuba player in the marching band. If I was Candy I would be afraid. He's got the look that Gwen has when she's about to go upside someone's head and hand out punishments.

He says, "Candy, if I have to pick you up and carry you in this house, you are going."

"If you touch me, I'm calling social services," Candy argues.

My eyebrows raise all the way to my hairline. This girl has got some guts on her! I wish I would tell Gwen I was calling the "people" on her. I'd be walking down the street right now trying to find my smacked off face.

Gwen whispers to me, "What is taking so long for them to come in?"

"I don't think his daughter wants to eat with us," I reply with a shrug.

Gwen frowns and gets that Neo from *The Matrix* look in her eye. Then, she says, "She better get her behind in this house. Ain't nobody playing with little Miss Candy."

Gwen sashays over to the door and calls out, "Come on in, you two! Dinner is getting cold."

Candy rolls her eyes like she doesn't have good sense. "No thank you. My *mother* fed me before I came."

I watch Gwen with much caution. I even back up a few steps because I'm not trying to get caught in the crossfire. Poor Elder LeRon looks so embarrassed, and I actually feel sorry for him.

My mother closes her eyes and takes a few deep breaths. Then, she puts a fake smile on her face and says, "Well, sweetie, I'm sure your mother is a great cook, so you don't have to eat anything if you don't want to. Just come on in, though, because it's getting cold outside."

Hush my mouth and call me turtle. I have never seen such a thing. Gwen is slipping for real.

Candy flashes her father a victorious look and marches up the walkway. Elder LeRon exhales slowly and sadly. Can anybody say *problem child*? That little heifer has issues.

Candy pushes me to the side as she walks through our front door. She looks around our home slowly, as if she's getting ready to write a report for her mama. Then this chick has the audacity to turn up her nose as if something stinks.

She says, "What is that smell? It smells like rotten barbeque sauce."

Oh no she didn't! No she did not. I cannot and I will not try to save her when Gwen punts her head across the room like a football.

"That would be dinner," Gwen replies. "And I guess it does smell a bit like barbeque sauce. It's my special recipe."

Candy laughs. "Boy, am I glad I already ate."

The Lord must have given Gwen an extra portion of grace and mercy for this day! I can't keep my mouth closed because it's hanging off the hinges with the shock of it all. I watch my mother smooth out her skirt and lead her man to the dinner table.

Believe it or not, I'm proud of Gwen.

Candy looks a little irritated that her father and my

mother are laughing and grinning in each other's faces. I hope she doesn't have too much more craziness up her sleeve, because Gwen may not last through another round of abuse.

"Is this where I'm supposed to sit?" Candy asks as she points at our couch as if it's a pile of garbage.

My eyes dart over to Gwen for her reply. "Honey, you can sit there if you want, or you can join us at the table."

"There's no way I'm sitting at your table. If I have to smell that food up close I just might get sick."

"Now, just wait a minute. . . ." Gwen says.

Looks like the grace and mercy just ran out.

Fortunately for Candy, Elder LeRon steps in. "Candy, you are going to stop acting like you don't have any home training. Apologize to Sister Gwen this instant."

"Or what?" Candy says.

"Or you're going to wish you were never born."

Candy sucks her teeth and rolls her eyes. "Yeah, right. I'm calling my mother right now. You can't make me do anything."

"Your mother is on a date with her new boyfriend, Candy. I'm sure she has turned her cell phone off."

Tears spring to Candy's eyes. She looks at the floor and plays with her hands. This is too much drama for our little house. Me and Gwen don't get down like this.

"I'm sorry," Candy says in a voice barely louder than a whisper.

"I'm sorry who?" Elder LeRon asks in a much calmer tone.

Candy sighs and says, "I'm sorry, Sister Gwen."

"I forgive you, honey," some crazy lady says. I'm not

saying Gwen because clearly we are dealing with some kind of *Body Snatchers* incident. I've never in all my days heard this many *honeys* and *sweeties* come up out of Gwen's mouth.

Elder LeRon walks across the room and takes Candy by the arm. He leads her over to the table and motions for her to sit. Then he says, "You will eat this meal that Sister Gwen has prepared for us. If you say one more thing out of order you will be grounded."

Candy plops down at the table and I sit down next to her. Directly across from us are our parents. I'm ashamed to say it, but I'm in awe of this little girl. I've never had the courage to speak my mind to Gwen, and if I had, it would've ended badly.

Elder LeRon blesses the food and Gwen starts the conversation.

"So," Gwen asks as she passes the bowl of spaghetti, "did you all hear about Ricardo in the Homecoming game? He was throwing that football clear across the field."

"It's about time! Coach Rogers has been sleeping on my boy," I say proudly.

Candy asks, "Your boy? Is he your boyfriend? You're allowed to have boyfriends?"

Okay, why is she all up in my business? It was cool when she was sparring with Gwen and her daddy, funny even. But she doesn't want to rumble with me.

"No," I reply indignantly. "Ricardo is not my boyfriend. He is my friend."

Elder LeRon says to my mother, "Ricky is a fine young man, but still it's best to be careful. We don't want another Romeo incident, do we?"

I'm about to lose my mind up in here. Since when did my life get to be dinner conversation? And when did anyone ask Elder LeRon his opinion about my scenarios? And now he's trying to be *my* daddy when his own daughter just punked him out in front of his future wife?

Gwen glances at me with an "I got this" look. Then she says, "Gia and I handled that situation. We don't need to rehash that ugliness tonight."

"I want to rehash it!" Candy exclaims. "What went down? Did you catch her and Romeo doing the do?"

The do? Wow on top of wow. It's taking every piece of salvation in me to keep from giving this child a piece of my mind. I'm keeping quiet for my mama.

"Candy, that was rude. You and Gia are going to be sisters, so I want you to treat her with respect," Elder LeRon says diplomatically.

"Hmph. She's not going to be my sister. She'll be your wife's daughter."

Was I just admiring this girl? I take it all back. She is the devil's spawn.

I reply, "Boo, the feeling is mutual. I've been an only child for fifteen years and that's the way I like it."

"Good!" Candy says.

"Girls, stop it!" Gwen yells.

Candy ignores her. "And I'm not sharing my room with you!"

"Good!" I snap back. "I wouldn't sleep within ten feet of you."

"Even better!" Candy hollers at the top of her lungs.

Gwen glares at Elder LeRon and asks, "Aren't you going to say anything?"

He nods. "Gwen, this spaghetti is really good."

That's what he has to say? For crying out loud! It looks like I'm in for some drama-filled days. If you know anything about prayer, can you please send one up for me and my mama?

★ 26 ★

Gwen's fiancé and his terrible child are now gone and it's just me and Gwen. She's been quiet ever since they left. I guess the evening didn't go exactly how she wanted. I'm sure Elder LeRon didn't prepare her for Candy. That girl is off the chain.

Gwen quietly clears the table and I straighten up the living room. It seems funny working in silence like this, but I do not want to start the conversation. I'll let Gwen bring it up if she wants to.

"Oh, Gia, I almost forgot to tell you," Gwen says. "I talked to Mrs. Vaughn yesterday."

"The Hi-Steppers coach? What did you talk to her about?" I ask hopefully.

"She was just telling me that you are a great asset to the team. She also said something about college scholar-ships."

Yay, Mrs. Vaughn! I knew she wasn't going to let me go that easily.

Gwen continues, "So, I was thinking about letting you rejoin the squad."

I jump up and hug Gwen around her neck. "Thank you, thank you, thank you, thank you, thank you, Mommy!"

"Wait a minute, before you get too excited. There are some conditions to this."

My eyebrows go up slowly. "What kind of conditions?"

"You may rejoin the squad, but there will be no Hi-Steppers sleepovers, no makeup, and no fake ponytails," Gwen says.

First of all, Gwen must not realize that I will not be invited to any more Hi-Steppers sleepovers, especially if they're at Valerie's house. If Valerie wasn't dissing me because of what happened with Romeo, she definitely will be now, after Ricky put her on serious blast.

The no makeup and no fake ponytail conditions are easy too. If I'm not hanging with Valerie, there's no need to compromise my current Afro-wearing fly girl status. She can keep her little plastic hair. I am so not the one.

"Do you think you can deal with that?" Gwen asks.

"Absolutely."

"I'm serious, Gia. Don't come begging me to go to anyone's house to spend the night."

"I can never go to sleepovers again? Ever?" I ask.

"Not until I can trust you again, Gia, and that's going to take a long time, I'm afraid."

I guess I understand where Gwen is coming from. I mean, I was tripping with all that lying and whatnot. I'm just glad that I'm still alive and in control of my senses. Gwen could've gone kung fu master on me and I could be eating through a straw. Yeah, it could happen.

A car pulls up outside and I run over to the window to see who it is. I hope it's not Elder LeRon and that problem teenager coming back to torture us some more. I pull the string on Gwen's prize vertical blinds so that I can see outside. It's not Elder LeRon at all. It's my uncle, Pastor Stokes. He, Hope, and Ricky are walking up to the house. Ricky and Hope still have on their Homecoming outfits.

"Open the door, Gia," Hope says from outside. "I see you looking out the window."

Laughing, I swing the door open so that they can enter. Hope's outfit is cute. She's wearing a Baby Phat dress with a jacket and leather boots. Ricky is wearing a blue sweater and baggy jeans and he tops off the look with Timberland boots. They both look good.

But why does Hope have her arm looped through Ricky's arm as if they're together? She's going to make me hurt her, I see. And we just got back on good terms too. Why, why, why?

I guess Hope sees me glaring at her, so she quickly untangles herself from Ricky. I wasn't the only one glaring, either. My uncle didn't look like he was too cool with that action.

Pastor Stokes walks over to my mother and gives her a hug. "Congratulations, Gwen. Hope told me about your engagement. Are you going to announce it at church?"

"Probably not," Gwen says. "No doubt those hateful sisters would just try to break us up! I'll announce it right before I get ready to walk down the aisle."

"Gwen! I'm pretty sure that Elder LeRon loves you and he can't be swayed by any hateful sisters," Pastor Stokes replies.

"Whatever," Gwen says. "You clearly have never been to one of our singles meetings. Those women are like vultures."

"Gwen, that's awful."

My mother shrugs and pulls Pastor Stokes toward the kitchen. "Come on, little brother. Let me make you some cocoa, and I'll tell you all about it."

When they're out of the room, Hope motions for me and Ricky to come into my bedroom. She plops down on my bed and Ricky sits in my beanbag chair. I just love how they are all up in my personal space, like I invited them or something.

Hope says, "Gia, aren't you going to ask us about the Homecoming dance?"

Did she just come over here to gloat about being at the dance while I was stuck at home? That's so not cool. I thought we were friends again.

"It was just a dance, right?"

Ricky laughs. "Right, Gia. It was just a dance, where Valerie got clowned big time."

Now, this I gotta hear. "Spill it!"

Ricky laughs. "Well, someone told Brad that Valerie was kicking it with me and some college dude she met at the rec center."

"I wonder who told him. Not too many people know about Valerie's dirt. She keeps that on the low-low," I say.

Hope replies, "Apparently, it was Jewel or Kelani. Both of them like Brad, so I can't say which one of them it was."

"So what happened?" I ask. "Don't keep a sista in suspense."

Ricky answers, "Brad confronted Valerie at the dance, right on the dance floor. He asked her if she was kicking it with me. Of course, she lied."

Hope interjects, "Then the best part happened! Brad took a glass of punch and poured it onto Valerie's white sweater."

"Wow! What did she do?"

Ricky laughs and says, "Well, you know Valerie. She wasn't having that, so she pushed him into the refreshment table and the punch bowl and all the snacks went crashing to the floor."

"Yikes. I bet everyone was tripping," I say.

"That wasn't the worst part," Hope says. "Valerie tried to walk away like she owned Brad and she slipped on some cake frosting. She went flying into the spilled food."

Oh, to have seen Valerie sprawled onto the floor with cake frosting in her hair and punch all over her clothes. I wish I could've been there for that.

I say, "That sounds crazy."

"Yeah, it was pretty wild," Ricky says. "I've never seen anyone get out on Valerie like that."

"Y'all want to hear some good news?" I ask.

Hope replies, "What, you saved money on your car insurance by switching to Geico?"

"Ha, ha. You're the opposite of funny, you know that?" Ricky laughs. "Gia, tell us your news."

"Mrs. Vaughn talked to Gwen about me rejoining the Hi-Steppers squad. Gwen said yes!"

Hope, for some reason, does not seem thrilled. "You're going back to the squad?"

"Yes, isn't that great?" I ask.

"I didn't think you would want to be a Hi-Stepper anymore after how Valerie played you," Hope says.

"Valerie is not the reason I joined the Hi-Steppers. I joined because I like stepping and it's completely hot!"

Hope laughs. "I thought you were trying to be popular."

"She was," Ricky says.

"Okay, yeah, I was trying to be popular too."

Hope replies, "We already know that, Gia. But I'm not rejoining the Hi-Steppers."

"You're not?" Ricky asks.

"Nah. It's not my cup of tea," Hope answers. "Gia's good at it, but I'm going to find something else that suits me."

"Like what?" I ask.

"I don't know. Maybe I'll be a rally girl, or a cheerleader. I don't know yet."

A rally girl or a cheerleader? Let me just say that both of those are bad choices. All bad. The rally girls are boy crazy and the cheerleaders are conceited snobs. Hope wouldn't be great in either circle. But I guess that's up to her to decide.

Ricky says, "I think you'd make a great rally girl."

Hope beams a smile over at him. "You do? That's the

one I was leaning toward. I think you just helped me make up my mind."

Can someone please tell me how long I'm going to have to endure Hope sweating Ricky? She's only interested in him because Valerie wanted him. All this smiling and flirting is getting completely out of control. They're going to make me have to regulate up in this piece.

And that would not be a good thing.

★ 27 ★

It is youth Sunday today at church. It's my favorite Sunday of the month because the youth choir gets to sing and the junior praise dancers get to dance. I'm especially pumped today because Hope and I are going to sing our joint solo.

"Gia, I wish you'd been at the Homecoming dance," Ricky says as we line up at the back of the sanctuary with the rest of the youth choir.

I draw my eyebrows together in a frown. "Really? According to Hope, the two of you had a blast without me. It sounds like you two were tee-hee-heeing all night."

Ricky smiles wistfully, like he's reminiscing. "We did have fun. Kevin came too."

"Kevin was at a dance?"

"Yep. He had a date too!"

My mouth falls open. "A date? You gotta be kidding me."

"Nah. Kevin brought some girl from the marching band," Ricky explains. "Her name is Patricia and she plays the clarinet."

"I just don't believe it! I can't and I won't."

"What? Is someone . . . I don't know . . . maybe . . . jealous?"

I throw my head back and laugh out loud. "No, absolutely not. Sir no sir."

I'm not jealous, but I gotta say that Jesus must be coming back soon if I'm sitting at the house while Bible-quoting Kevin is getting play. That must be a sign of the end times.

Brother Bryan walks up and down next to our line and smiles proudly. He says, "You all look great in that navy blue and gray! Does anyone have any prayer requests before we minister to the congregation in song?"

Hope raises her hand. "I don't have a prayer request, but I do have a praise report!"

Brother Bryan nods and says, "Go ahead, Sister Stokes. Tell us what's on your heart."

Hope clears her throat and says, "I just want to thank God because my cousin and I are friends again. I've been so mean to her since this past summer, but she's always had my back. And . . . umm . . . I'm just glad we're friends again."

As if her words haven't shocked me enough, she walks over and gives me a crazy big hug! I can hardly believe this is real. But then Ricky walks over and wraps his arms around both of us and squeezes hard. It *is* real.

Hope whispers in my ear, "Let's never fight again, okay?"

"Okay," I answer, trying not to let her hear that I'm all choked up.

I don't want us to be enemies anymore. I most definitely need all the friends I can get. Especially when one of the Children of the Corn is about to be my baby stepsister.

We march into the church after Pastor Stokes says the opening prayer. Everyone claps and stomps as we walk down the center aisle, because the young people get crunk like that on youth Sunday.

When we all get into the choir stand, Brother Bryan steps to the microphone. "Are y'all ready to praise the Lord with us this morning?" he asks.

Everyone in the church replies by clapping and shouting. Brother Bryan smiles and then signals to the musicians to start our song.

Hope grips the microphone tightly and closes her eyes. Then, she follows the lead of the music and starts to sing. She sounds better than I've ever heard her sound. The choir also sounds great and completely on key.

When we get to the bridge part of the song, Hope hands me her microphone. I open my mouth and let loose the voice that God gave me. Then Hope is standing next to me harmonizing with every note.

Nearly half the congregation is standing and clapping and praising God. Me singing with Hope is awesome. Actually . . . it's the stuff of legends.

STEP TO THIS

Nikki Carter

ABOUT THIS GUIDE

The following questions are intended to
enhance your group's reading of
STEP TO THIS.

Discussion Questions

1. What do you think of Gia's style? Hot? Or NOT? What is unique about your own style?

2. How did you feel when Gia made the Hi-Steppers B squad? Did you think she handled her disappointment well? How do you deal with total letdowns?

3. Is Valerie a mean girl? Why or why not? What did you think about the way she treated Ricky?

4. In the beginning of the story, Gia is sad about her ex-friendship status with Hope. Have you ever lost a BFF? What do you do when that happens?

5. Do you know anyone like Jewel and Kelani? Do you love them or do they totally irk you? Why or why not?

6. Did you know what Romeo was about from day one? Why do you think Gia was fooled?

7. Should Gia give clammy-hands Kevin a chance? Why or why not?

8. On Gia's date with Romeo he tries to make her do things she's uncomfortable with. Have you ever

been in an awkward situation with a boy? How did you deal with it?

9. After Gia and Romeo's date, he treats her badly at school. What did you think of how she handled it?

10. If you were in Gia's shoes, would you forgive Romeo or get revenge? Why or why not?

11. Did Romeo and Valerie get what they deserved?

12. What do you think is next for Gia?

A Discussion with the Author

1. **Coke or Pepsi?**
Pepsi.

2. **What are your favorite TV Shows?**
Friday Night Lights, Smallville, Grey's Anatomy,
and *Heroes* (Save the cheerleader, save the
world!!! Yeah!).

3. **Bath or shower?**
Both.

4. **What's your most embarrassing moment?**
I was at a house party in my good friend's base-
ment. I went upstairs to get a snack and when I
headed back downstairs, I slipped and fell down
the flight of stairs. The music stopped, but I just
hopped up and started dancing. Trust . . . it was
ALL bad!

5. **Who's your favorite actress?**
Sanaa Lathan! *Love and Basketball* is one of my
favorite movies!

6. **Who's your favorite actor?**
I have more than one. Johnny Depp, Denzel Washington, and Idris Elba!

7. **Who's your favorite singer?**
   This changes a lot. Right now, I'm feeling Beyoncé, Alicia Keys, and Jennifer Hudson. I also like fun gospel artists like KiKi Sheard.

`8. **Have you ever been in love?**
   Yes!

9. **If you could be a celeb for a day, who would you be?**
   Hmm . . . Kimora Lee! She is running thangs. So fabulous!

10. **Flip-flops or Crocs?**
    Umm . . . neither.

11. **What lesson should readers learn from *Step to This*?**
    The lesson is that it's okay to be unique and fearless! You can be a Christian and fab. Also, the people who appreciate you for doing YOU are the ones that you want in your life!

Want more?
Check out
IT IS WHAT IT IS
by Nikki Carter.
Available in July 2009
wherever books are sold.

Are bridesmaid dresses supposed to itch?

I'm asking because my mom, Gwen, has me standing in front of the church wearing a ridiculous amount of pink taffeta and some other material that's making me itch. I close one eye and try to concentrate on making the itch disappear, because it's in the center of my back, right where I can't reach it.

The concentration isn't working, so I shift my shoulders in little circles trying to reach the itch with the zipper on my dress.

"Will you *stop* it?" my cousin Hope hisses. "Auntie Gwen is gonna get you when she sees you squirming on her wedding video."

She's right. Gwen will be heated. But it's her own fault. She shouldn't have picked outfits that make us look like Destiny's Child backup dancers. All of this shining and glistening is a bit extra if you ask me.

Even though I'm sixteen and on my way into the eleventh grade, this is Gwen's first wedding. She met a guy at our church named Elder LeRon Ferguson and they really hit it off. Even the pastor (who is also my uncle) was happy about them getting together. On the real, I think the only two people *not* happy about this whole blessed affair are me and Elder LeRon's daughter, Candy.

Don't get it twisted, I want my mother to be happy, get a man and all that, but I just thought it would all take place after I was grown. I am so not in the mood for a new dad and a bratty little sister who will probably make my life miserable.

But if Gwen's going to get upset if she sees me trying to scratch my itch, then she's gonna be extra heated when she sees Candy on video. She practically stomped down the aisle and didn't even hold her flower bouquet up in front of her. She let her arms drop to her sides and mean-mugged the video guy all the way to the front of the church.

This itch is really starting to drive me nuts. This whole wedding ceremony thing is taking forever, too! Gwen had to go all out and have three flower girls and a miniature bride. I mean, for real, is all that even necessary?

As the third flower girl marches up the aisle throwing flowers everywhere but the floor in front of her, Hope leans forward and whispers, "There's Ricky."

We both smile at *my* best friend, Ricardo. Umm . . . yeah . . . survey says no. Hope needs to pause all of that action immediately. She's been lightweight digging Ricky ever since Homecoming of last year. And that's only because he got upgraded to "hot" status by Longfellow High's resident vixen, Valerie. She's the captain of the Hi-Steppers squad and not exactly my favorite person.

Ricky smiles back at us and waves. Even though I'm standing in front of the church, I can tell he's looking real fresh and real clean. My mom would say he looks dapper in his church suit and tie. But I ain't Gwen and *dapper* is a word from those old movies.

I know what you're thinking, and the answer is no! Ricky is just my friend, not my *boyfriend*. Gwen is dead set against me dating until I'm in college. This is not an exaggeration either. I totally wish I was exaggerating.

Finally, Gwen starts marching up the center aisle of the church. It's about time! When the entire congregation turns to watch her, I take my bouquet and try to scratch my back with the little plastic holder thingy.

My mom looks real pretty, kinda like me but older. She's grinning from ear to ear as everyone takes pictures of her. Since her only close male family member is my uncle, Pastor Stokes, she decided to walk down the aisle alone.

When I asked if Pastor was going to give her away, these were her exact words: "I'm a grown woman, and I belong to God. I'm giving myself away."

Oh, the bluntness.

I am glad when Gwen makes her way up the three little steps to stand in front of the pastor and next to Elder LeRon. She looks real fly in her off-the-shoulder bridal gown that me and Hope helped her pick out. Aunt Elena helped too, but she's my uncle's wife and Gwen isn't really feeling her.

Pastor Stokes starts up with his standard wedding sermon. He's talking about love, forgiveness, and all kinds of stuff I don't need to worry about right now. My new stepsister, Candy, sighs loudly like she's bored out of her mind. But Gwen gives her some serious I-will-cut-you-if-you-mess-up-my-wedding-day side eye and she pulls herself together quickly.

After the vows are exchanged, and Elder LeRon kisses my mom, the ceremony ends, although we have to stand up here letting everyone in the church hug and kiss us. I am so not feeling that. I've got about fifty different shades of lipstick smeared on my face, and everyone's breath is not fresh. I mean, if you're gonna eat an onion and pickle sandwich, you can at least respect the personal space perimeter or get yourself some extra-strength Altoids. For real.

Speaking of people who don't respect personal space, clammy-hands Kevin is standing in line with his grandparents. Kevin has been in love with me for like ever, and trust, it is completely against my will. And why did he just wink at me? Boy, bye!

"Here comes your boyfriend," Hope teases.

Candy overhears and scrunches up her nose. "That's your boyfriend? You have horrible taste."

"Kevin is not my boyfriend," I argue. "Hope is the one who went out on a date with him."

Hope pinches the back of my arm and frowns. She would love to forget her "date" with Kevin. It was really supposed to be my first date with a football player named Romeo. But Hope was in straight hater mode, ended up crashing and had to chill with Kevin for the evening. Let's just say that was not a fun outing for Hope.

Actually, even though Kevin is the opposite of everything fab, he is a whole lot better than Romeo. Months have gone by but I'm still somewhat irritated about how Romeo played me. You don't easily get over a boy taking you out on a date and leaving you stranded at the beach, just because you won't get freaky with him.

I know that Jesus would forgive him, but I'm still getting there, okay?

Kevin finally makes it through the line and hugs everyone, including me. "Gia, you look really pretty."

"Thank you, Kevin," I reply with a tight smile.

I almost said something smart, but I'm practicing accepting compliments graciously. And if I do say so myself, outside of this pink, frilly monstrosity, I do look kinda hot! My hair is especially fresh because Gwen gave me a two-stranded twist-out.

I see you giving me a blank stare, so let me explain. My mom washed my hair and then put cream and gel in and twisted it down my back until it dried. Then, she untwisted it and let the waves hang down on one side and pinned it up in the back.

Yeah, reread that and take a mental picture. Just trust me, okay? It's fly.

Next in the line is Ricky. Hope reaches ahead of me and hugs *my* best friend. I think I need to keep saying that, because Hope doesn't seem to understand. She's trying my patience.

Then Ricky hugs me too. "Are we going skating after the reception?"

"You know it!" I reply, and give my boy a high-five.

Hope frowns at me. "Do you think you could act like a lady for five minutes?"

I roll my eyes at Hope and ask Ricky, "Can you scratch my back?"

"Gia!" Hope exclaims.

Ricky and I crack up laughing because we know this irritates Hope. Hope and I have only recently renewed our BFF status. We went through some drama during our freshman and sophomore years, but we're cool now.

Even though we're friends again, we have very different ideas on what is fab and what isn't fab. Hope thinks that wearing designer clothes and making sure her lip gloss matches her purse is fly. The only matching I do is to make sure I have on two of the same socks. Outside of that, it's a free-for-all.

Finally, it's time to head over to the church social hall for the wedding reception. Gwen got Sister Benjamin from the kitchen ministry at church to cater, and I'm getting super hungry thinking about her fried chicken and sugar yams. I'm about to get my serious grub on.

Hope, Candy, and I sit at the wedding party table waiting for our food to be brought by the servers. I'm in chill mode, but Candy is looking like a straight hater with her arms crossed and her face pulled into a haterific frown.

"What's wrong with you, Candy?" Hope asks.

Candy looks Hope up and down and says, "Mind ya' bidness."

"Ugh," Hope replies. "You would be cute if you weren't so evil."

"And you would be cute if . . . well, nah, that would never happen," Candy says.

Can I just say that I agree with Hope? Candy has long, thick hair that she wears in a braid down the back of her head. Her eyes are big and pretty too, and she's got smooth dark brown skin with not even one pimple.

But Hope is right. Candy is not just evil . . . she's super duper evil.

I never thought I'd meet anyone as sarcastic as me, but Candy has got me beat for real. Anytime she opens her mouth an insult comes out of it. Even if you say something nice to her, she gives off nothing but negativity.

It's not a good look.

"I'm going skating with you," Candy says as if it's true.

"Umm . . . no you're not," I reply.

She lets out an evil cackle. "Oh, yes I am. I already asked your mother and she said that you had to let me come."

What! We'll see about this. I march right on down to the other end of the table where the new Mrs. Ferguson is grinning and cheesing. Yeah, she can calm all of that down, because we need to have a conference.

I tap Gwen on the shoulder and she looks up. "Hi, sweetie, the food will be out in a minute."

"Okay, but did you tell Candy that she could go skating with me and Ricky?"

She pauses for a moment like she's trying to remember. Then she says, "Yes, I think I did. LeRon and I think you two should get to know each other, since you'll be living under the same roof."

"Mom, that's not fair. She's not even nice, and I don't want her around my friends." I know I'm whining, but I really am not feeling this.

Gwen frowns. "Too bad. She's your new sister and sisters stick together."

"But Mom!"

"Deal with it, Gi... Gwen fusses. "Don't make me get ugly with you on ... ay. You are about to make me mess up my ...

Elder LeRo... ...her and asks, "Is everythin... ...frowning?"

Gwen ...

anythin...

So, ...and eat ... ...extra cri... ...situati... ...ng there with a...

Candy lea... ...Gia. Your mother wants me... ...g to do anything I ask. The two o... ...ave lots of fun this year."

Why do I get the feeling that her i... a of fun is my idea of torture?

head. Her eyes are big and pretty too, and she's got smooth dark brown skin with not even one pimple.

But Hope is right. Candy is not just evil . . . she's super duper evil.

I never thought I'd meet anyone as sarcastic as me, but Candy has got me beat for real. Anytime she opens her mouth an insult comes out of it. Even if you say something nice to her, she gives off nothing but negativity.

It's not a good look.

"I'm going skating with you," Candy says as if it's true.

"Umm . . . no you're not," I reply.

She lets out an evil cackle. "Oh, yes I am. I already asked your mother and she said that you had to let me come."

What! We'll see about this. I march right on down to the other end of the table where the new Mrs. Ferguson is grinning and cheesing. Yeah, she can calm all of that down, because we need to have a conference.

I tap Gwen on the shoulder and she looks up. "Hi, sweetie, the food will be out in a minute."

"Okay, but did you tell Candy that she could go skating with me and Ricky?"

She pauses for a moment like she's trying to remember. Then she says, "Yes, I think I did. LeRon and I think you two should get to know each other, since you'll be living under the same roof."

"Mom, that's not fair. She's not even nice, and I don't want her around my friends." I know I'm whining, but I really am not feeling this.

Gwen frowns. "Too bad. She's your new sister and sisters stick together."

"But Mom!"

"Deal with it, Gia!" Gwen fusses. "Don't make me get ugly with you on my wedding day. You are about to make me mess up my makeup."

Elder LeRon sits down next to my mother and asks, "Is everything all right, Gwenie? Gia, why are you frowning?"

Gwen gives me a look that says, *You better not say anything.*

So, I don't. I go back down to our end of the table and eat my food in silence. Not even Sister Benjamin's extra crispy chicken and sugary yams are improving the situation. And Candy isn't making it any better, sitting there with a smirk on her face.

Candy leans over and whispers, "I told you, Gia. Your mother wants me to like her and she's going to do anything I ask. The two of us are going to have lots of fun this year."

Why do I get the feeling that her idea of fun is my idea of torture?